my Li[...] PO[...]

Friendship is Magic

My Little Pony™ Friendship is Magic

WRITTEN BY
Katie Cook

ART BY
Andy Price

COLORS BY
Heather Breckel

LETTERS BY
Robbie Robbins

EDITED BY
Bobby Curnow

COVER BY
Stephanie Buscema

DIGEST EDITS BY
Justin Eisinger & Alonzo Simon

DIGEST DESIGN BY
Neil Uyetake

For Grayson, my own lil' Cutie Mark Crusader. -Katie

With great love to friends and family, for my wife Alice and our cats Spooky, Tabitha, Boris, Bela, and Mina. And above all, especially for Sam. -Andy

Special thanks to Erin Comella, Robert Fewkes, Heather Hopkins, Valerie Jurries, Ed Lane, Brian Lenard, Marissa Mansolillo, Donna Tobin, Michael Vogel, Mark Wiesenhahn, and Michael Kelly for their invaluable assistance.

IDW founded by Ted Adams, Alex Garner, Kris Oprisko, and Robbie Robbins

ISBN: 978-1-61377-628-5

16 15 14 13 1 2 3 4

IDW Licensed By: Hasbro

Ted Adams, CEO & Publisher
Greg Goldstein, President & COO
Robbie Robbins, EVP/Sr. Graphic Artist
Chris Ryall, Chief Creative Officer/Editor-in-Chief
Matthew Ruzicka, CPA, Chief Financial Officer
Alan Payne, VP of Sales
Dirk Wood, VP of Marketing
Lorelei Bunjes, VP of Digital Services

Become our fan on Facebook **facebook.com/idwpublishing**
Follow us on Twitter **@idwpublishing**
Check us out on YouTube **youtube.com/idwpublishing**
www.IDWPUBLISHING.com

Originally published as MY LITTLE PONY: FRIENDSHIP IS MAGIC Issues #1–2.

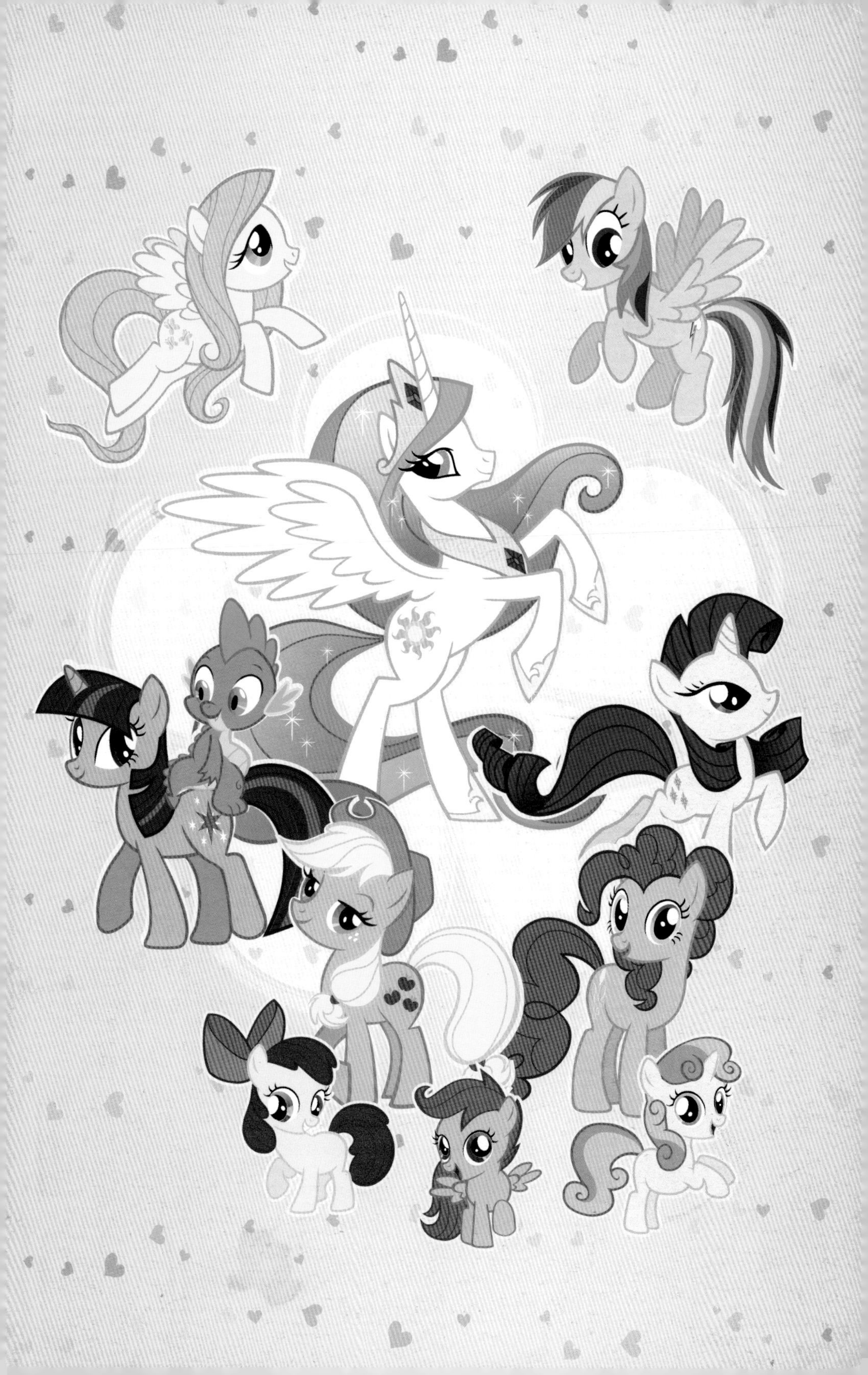

TWILIGHT SPARKLE

Twilight Sparkle is a unicorn with a big heart. Even though she prefers to have her muzzle stuck in a book, she's always willing to put her work aside to help her friends! She's also one of the most magically gifted unicorns there is thanks to her studies and the personal guidance of Princess Celestia.

RARITY

Rarity is a unicorn who has dedicated her life to making beautiful things... She's a fashion designer in Ponyville and has aspirations to be "the biggest thing in Equestria." She has big dreams, but she's very dedicated to her Ponyville friends who have always been there for her.

FLUTTERSHY

Fluttershy is a shy pegasus with a gentle hoof. Her love and understanding of animals is almost legendary to the ponies around her. She's calm and collected, even when faced with some of the scariest beings in the Everfree Forest!

APPLEJACK

Applejack is a pony you can trust. She's the hardest worker in all of Ponyville and will always be there to lend a helping hoof! She and her family run Sweet Apple Acres, the foremost place to acquire apples and apple-related goodies in Ponyville.

PINKIE PIE

Pinkie Pie is a pony that likes to PAR-TAY. Friendly, funny... and maybe a little weird, Pinkie Pie is always 'on hoof' for a celebration for any occasion! She's always there with a smile and an elaborate cake, even if she's just saying "thanks for pet-sitting my alligator."

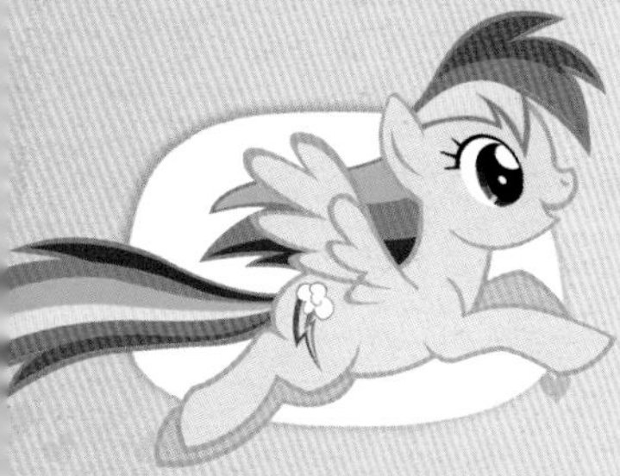

RAINBOW DASH

Rainbow Dash is the fastest pegasus around... and she KNOWS it! Never one to turn down a challenge, she's always ready to seize the day (in the spirit of friendly competition of course!).

SPIKE

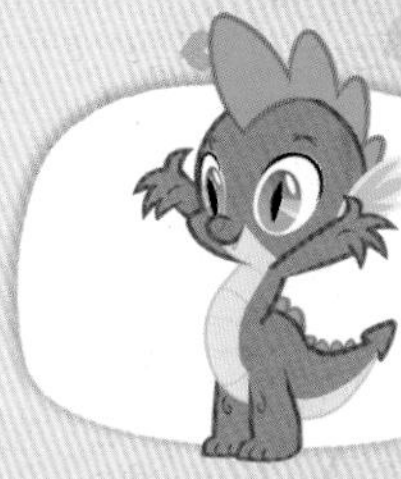

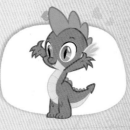

Spike the Dragon is the pint-sized assistant to Twilight Sparkle. Besides helping her out in the Ponyville library, he helps her practice spells and the duties of her daily life... he may be in the designated role of "helper," but he's also her dear friend.

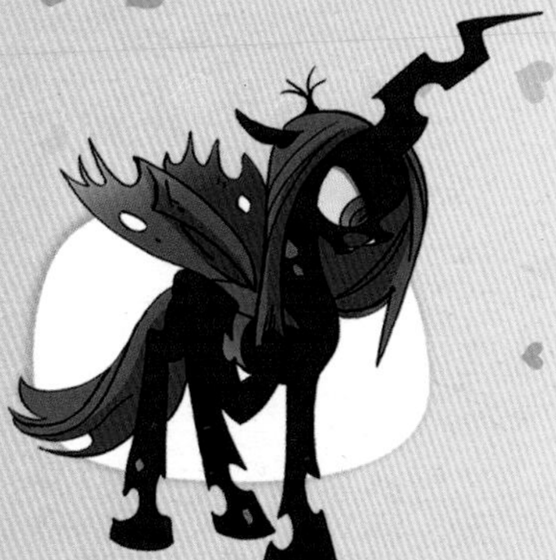

QUEEN CHRYSALIS

Queen Chrysalis is the Queen of the Changelings. After a failed attempt to take over Equestria, she now has her sights set on Twilight and her friends.

PRINCESS CELESTIA

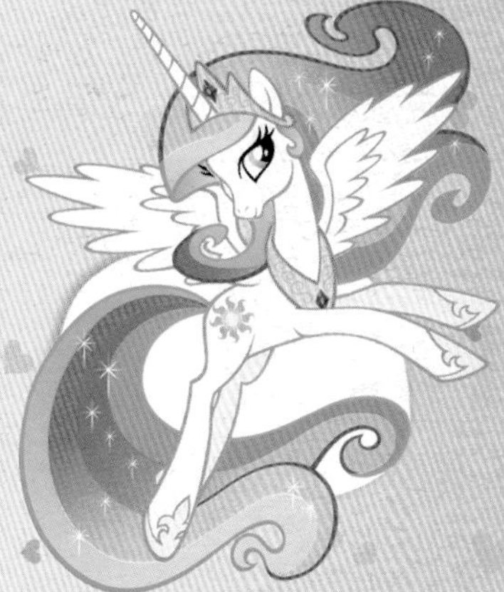

Princess Celestia is the ruler of Equestria and Twilight Sparkle's mentor. Princess Celestia is kind, gentle, and powerful... everything she needs to be to rule and protect her kingdom.

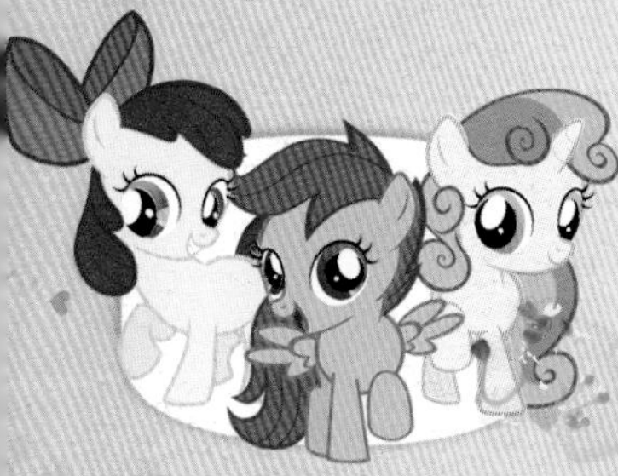

THE CUTIE MARK CRUSADERS

The Cutie Mark Crusaders are comprised of Sweetie Belle, Apple Bloom, and Scootaloo. These young fillies have yet to earn their cutie marks (the image on a pony's flank depicting their special talent!) and they are dashing through task after task together with the sole purpose of finding what makes them unique.

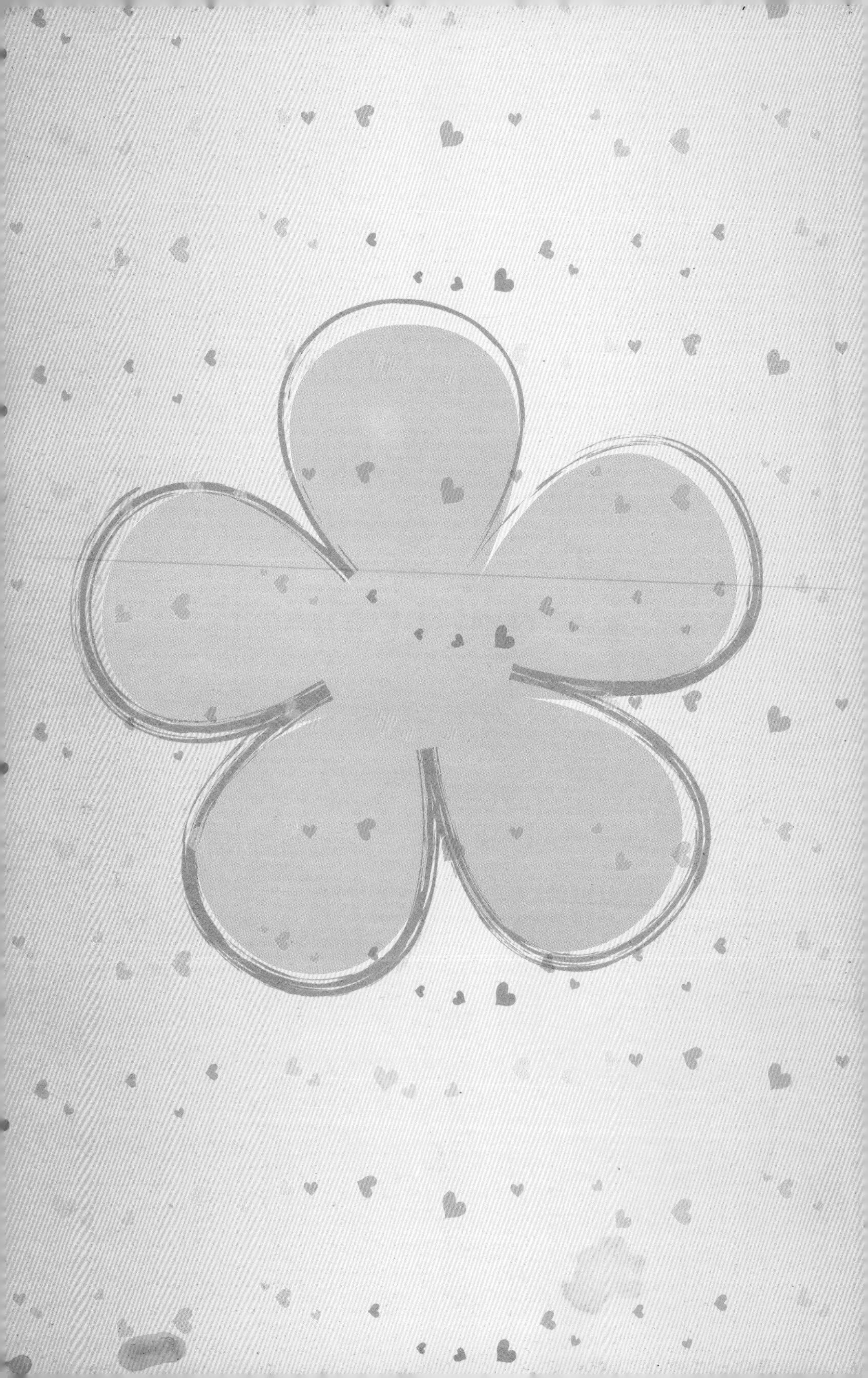

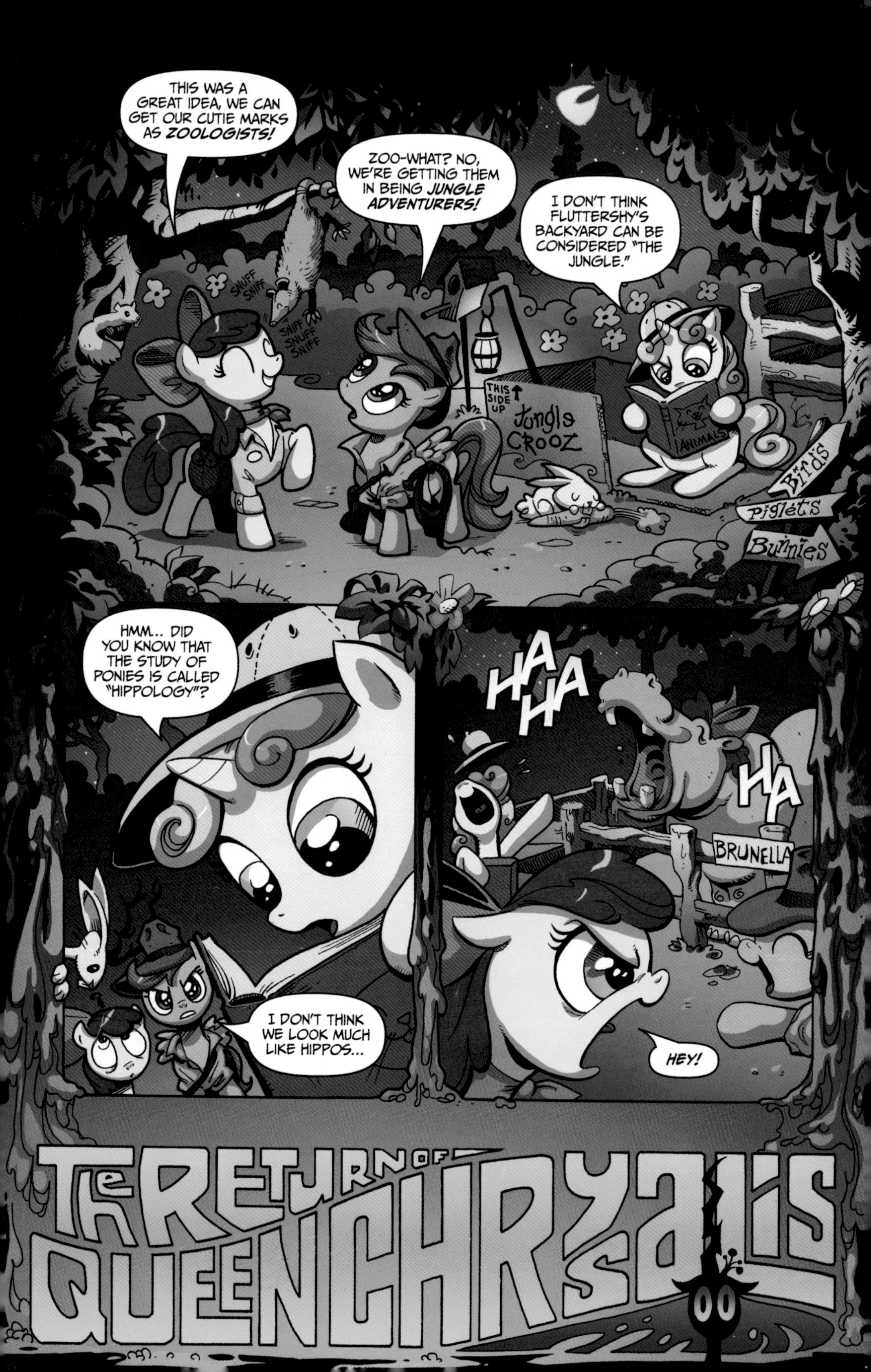
THIS WAS A GREAT IDEA, WE CAN GET OUR CUTIE MARKS AS ZOOLOGISTS!
SNUFF SNIFF
SNIFF SNUFF SNIFF
ZOO-WHAT? NO, WE'RE GETTING THEM IN BEING JUNGLE ADVENTURERS!
I DON'T THINK FLUTTERSHY'S BACKYARD CAN BE CONSIDERED "THE JUNGLE."
THIS SIDE UP
Jungle CROOZ
ANIMALS
Birds
Piglet's
Bunnies
HMM... DID YOU KNOW THAT THE STUDY OF PONIES IS CALLED "HIPPOLOGY"?
I DON'T THINK WE LOOK MUCH LIKE HIPPOS...
HA HA HA
HA
BRUNELLA
HEY!
THE RETURN OF QUEEN CHRYSALIS

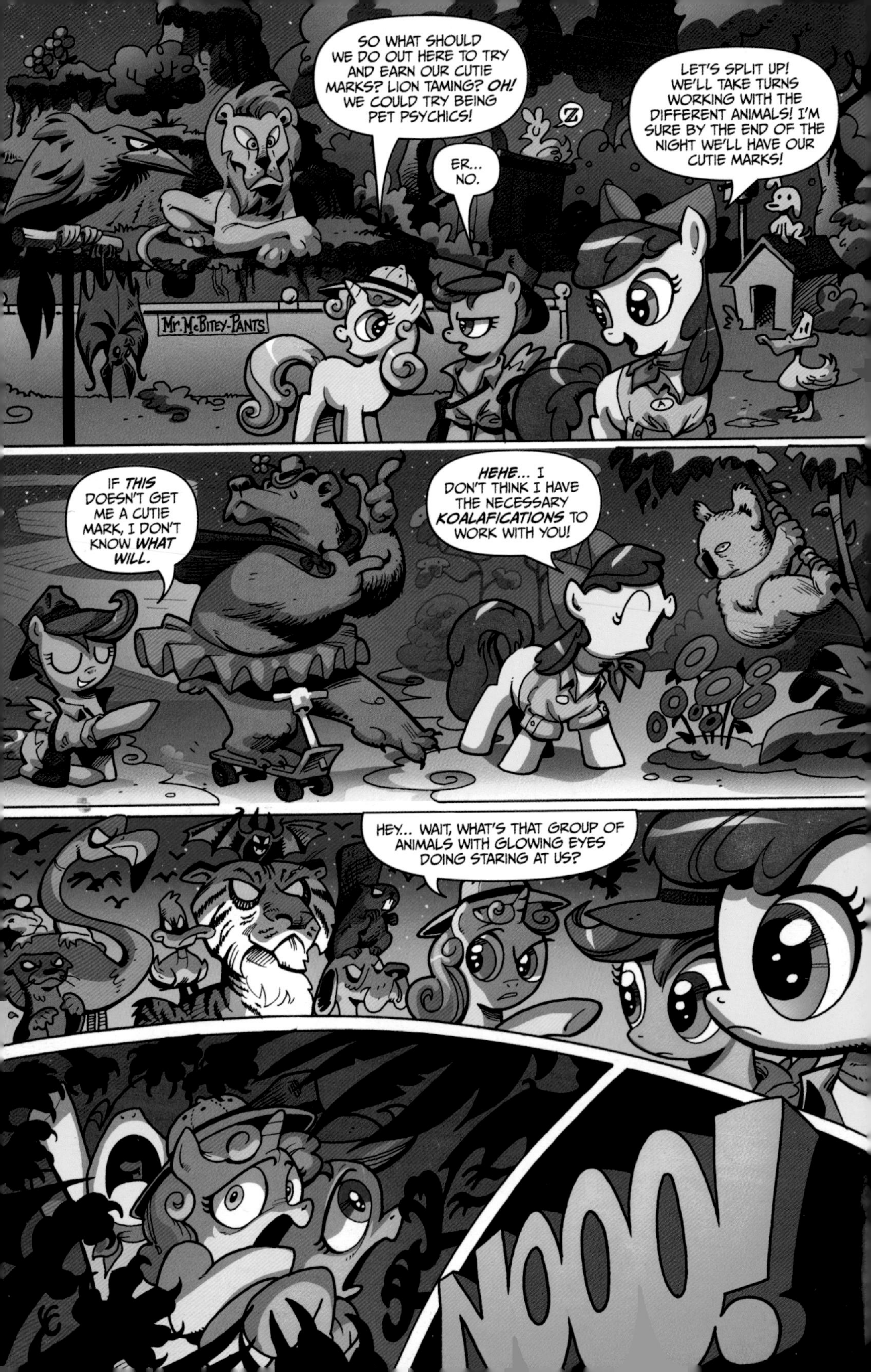

SO WHAT SHOULD WE DO OUT HERE TO TRY AND EARN OUR CUTIE MARKS? LION TAMING? OH! WE COULD TRY BEING PET PSYCHICS!
ER... NO.
LET'S SPLIT UP! WE'LL TAKE TURNS WORKING WITH THE DIFFERENT ANIMALS! I'M SURE BY THE END OF THE NIGHT WE'LL HAVE OUR CUTIE MARKS!
MR. MCBITEY-PANTS
IF THIS DOESN'T GET ME A CUTIE MARK, I DON'T KNOW WHAT WILL.
HEHE... I DON'T THINK I HAVE THE NECESSARY KOALAFICATIONS TO WORK WITH YOU!
HEY... WAIT, WHAT'S THAT GROUP OF ANIMALS WITH GLOWING EYES DOING STARING AT US?
NOOO!

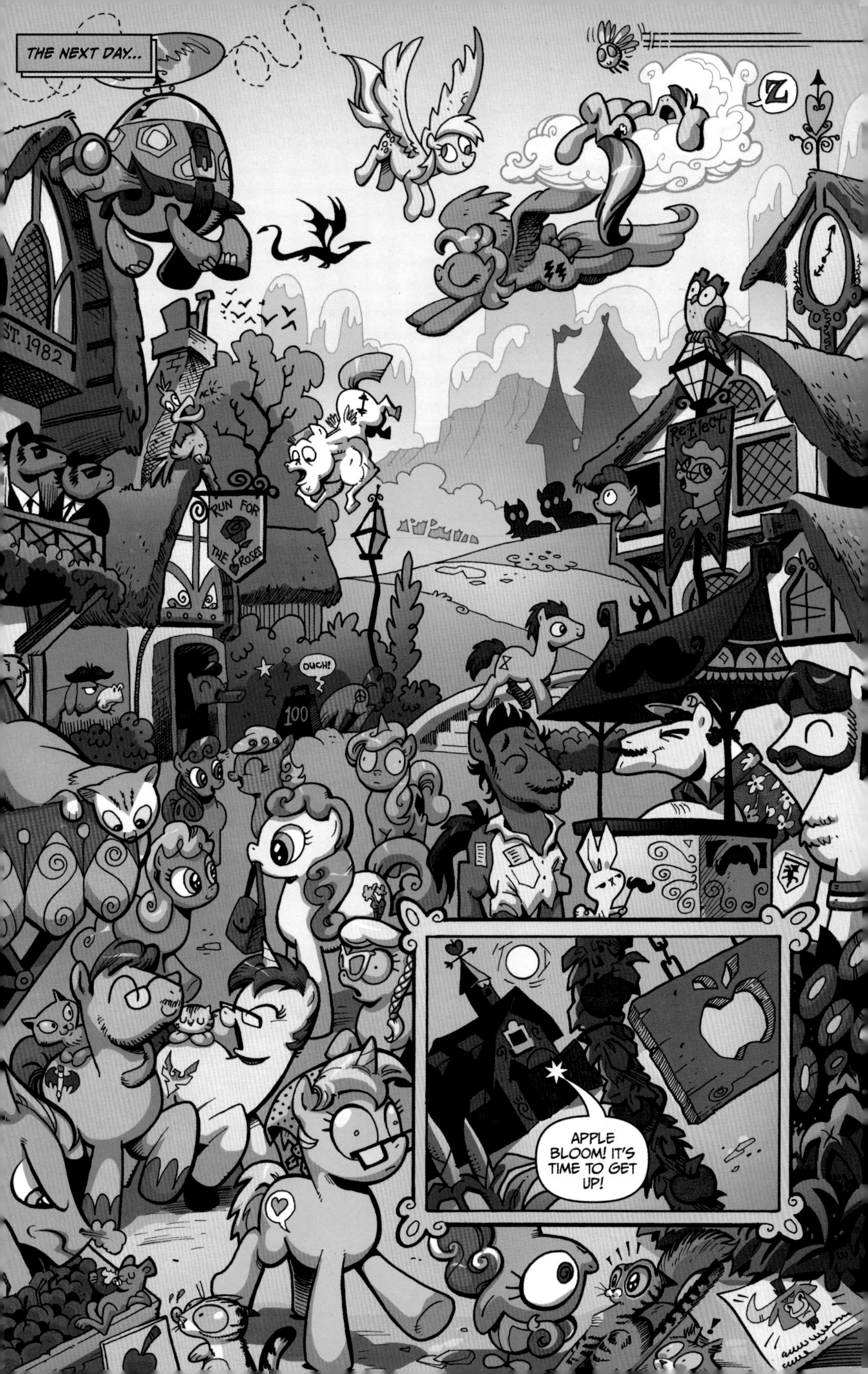
THE NEXT DAY...
Z
EST. 1982
ACK
RUN FOR THE ROSES
Re-Elect
OUCH!
100
APPLE BLOOM! IT'S TIME TO GET UP!

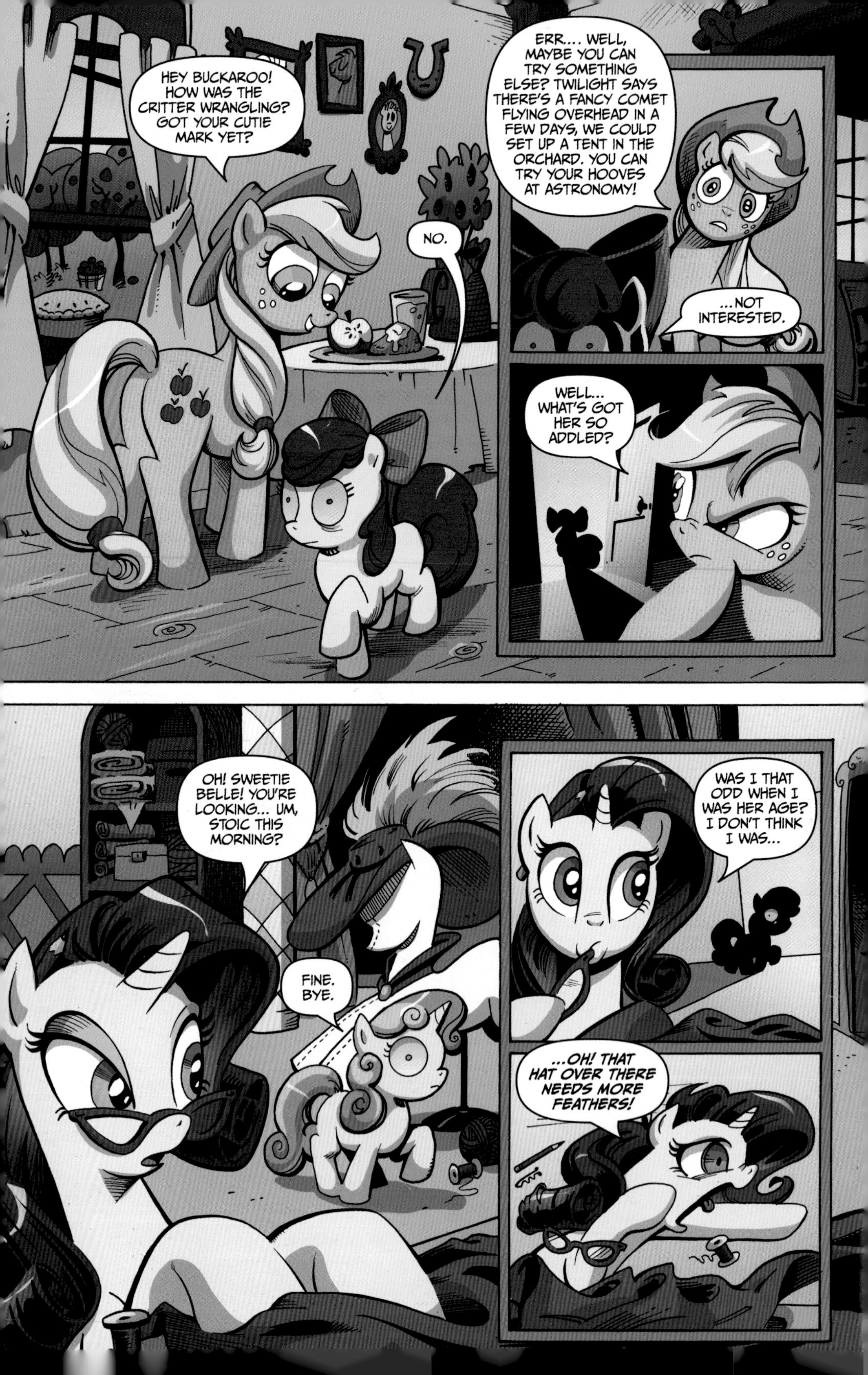

HEY BUCKAROO! HOW WAS THE CRITTER WRANGLING? GOT YOUR CUTIE MARK YET?
NO.
ERR.... WELL, MAYBE YOU CAN TRY SOMETHING ELSE? TWILIGHT SAYS THERE'S A FANCY COMET FLYING OVERHEAD IN A FEW DAYS, WE COULD SET UP A TENT IN THE ORCHARD. YOU CAN TRY YOUR HOOVES AT ASTRONOMY!
...NOT INTERESTED.
WELL... WHAT'S GOT HER SO ADDLED?
OH! SWEETIE BELLE! YOU'RE LOOKING... UM, STOIC THIS MORNING?
FINE. BYE.
WAS I THAT ODD WHEN I WAS HER AGE? I DON'T THINK I WAS...
...OH! THAT HAT OVER THERE NEEDS MORE FEATHERS!

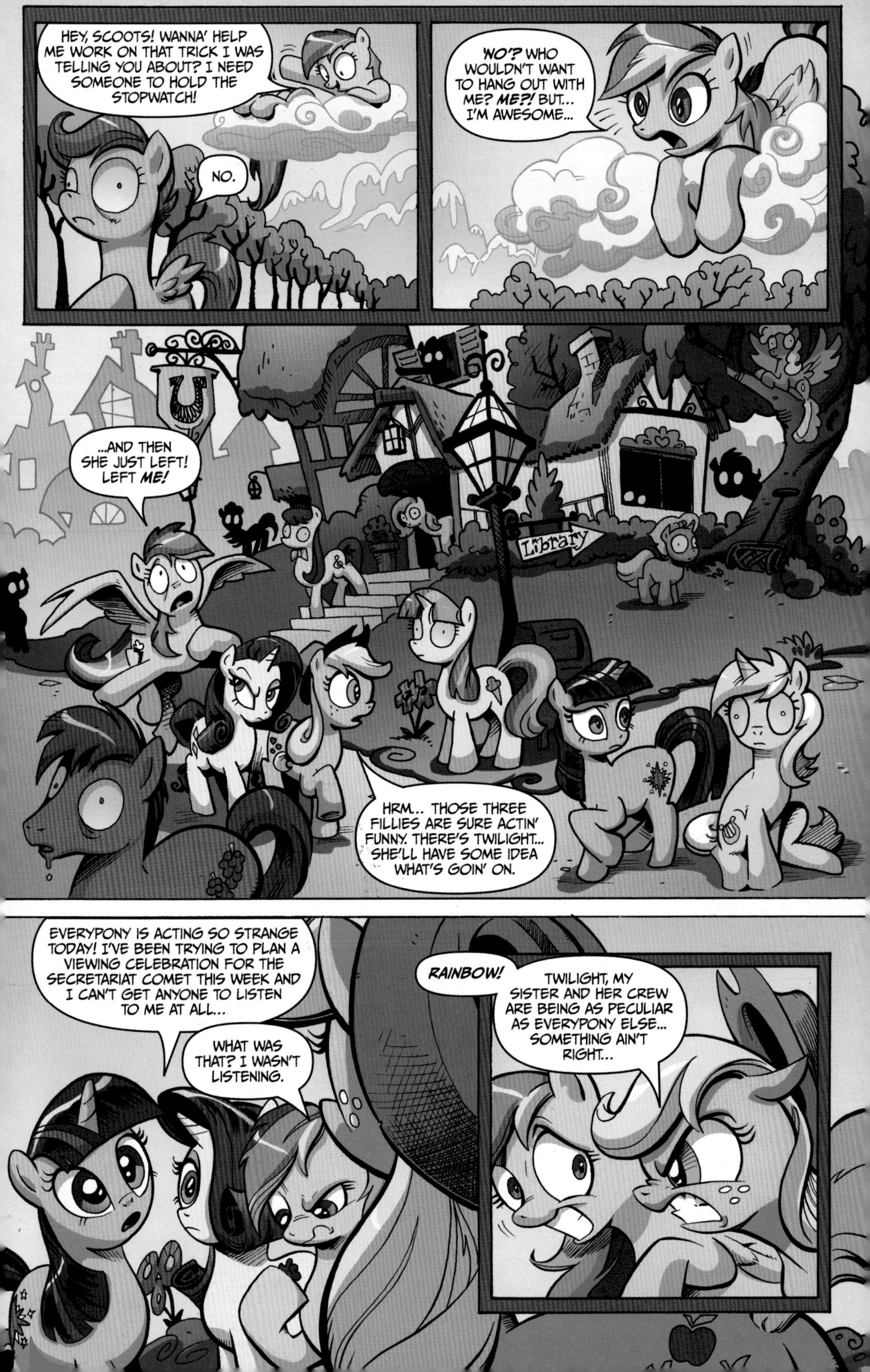
HEY, SCOOTS! WANNA' HELP ME WORK ON THAT TRICK I WAS TELLING YOU ABOUT? I NEED SOMEONE TO HOLD THE STOPWATCH!
NO.
'NO'? WHO WOULDN'T WANT TO HANG OUT WITH ME? ME?! BUT... I'M AWESOME...
...AND THEN SHE JUST LEFT! LEFT ME!
Library
HRM... THOSE THREE FILLIES ARE SURE ACTIN' FUNNY. THERE'S TWILIGHT... SHE'LL HAVE SOME IDEA WHAT'S GOIN' ON.
EVERYPONY IS ACTING SO STRANGE TODAY! I'VE BEEN TRYING TO PLAN A VIEWING CELEBRATION FOR THE SECRETARIAT COMET THIS WEEK AND I CAN'T GET ANYONE TO LISTEN TO ME AT ALL...
WHAT WAS THAT? I WASN'T LISTENING.
RAINBOW!
TWILIGHT, MY SISTER AND HER CREW ARE BEING AS PECULIAR AS EVERYPONY ELSE... SOMETHING AIN'T RIGHT...

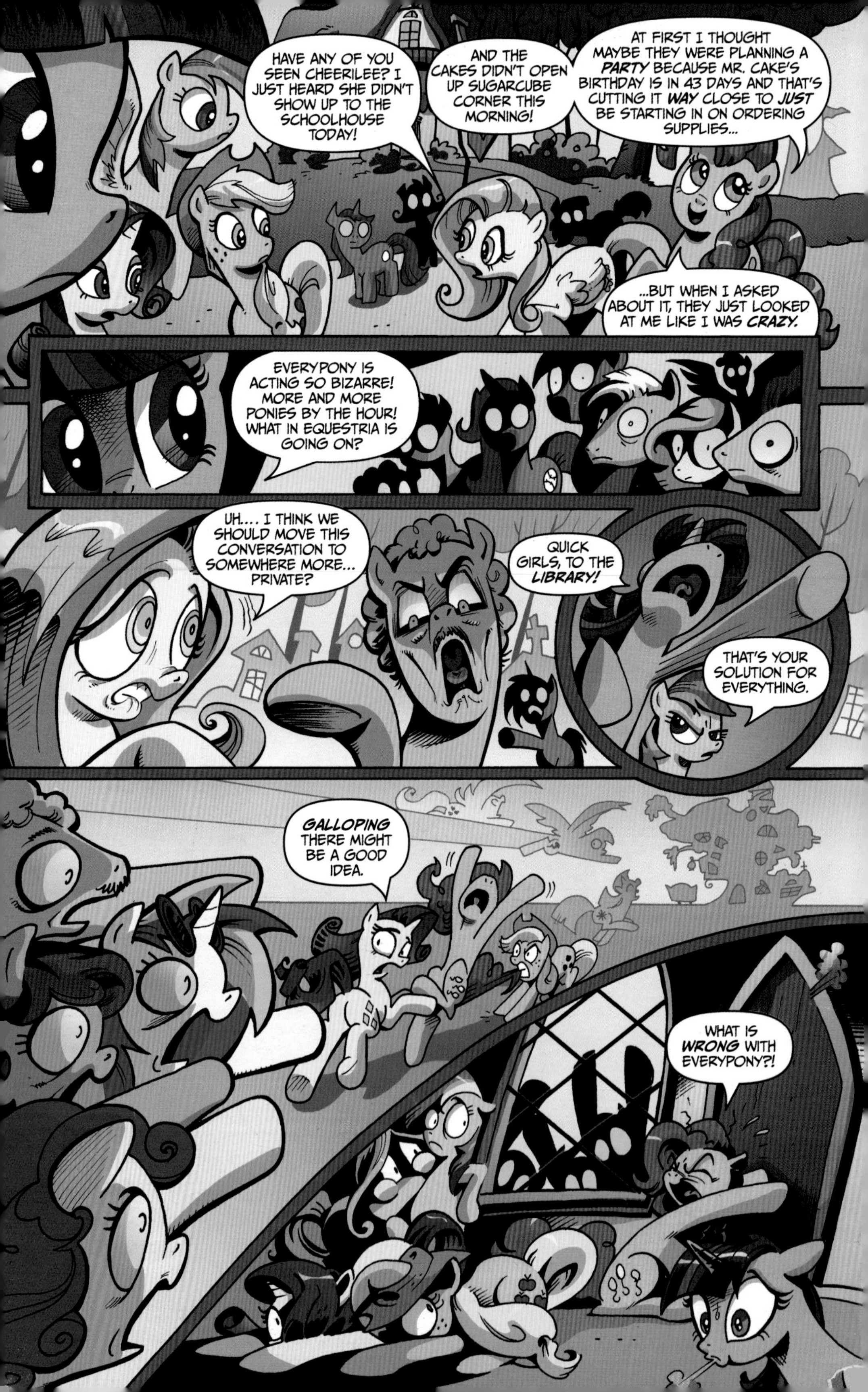
HAVE ANY OF YOU SEEN CHEERILEE? I JUST HEARD SHE DIDN'T SHOW UP TO THE SCHOOLHOUSE TODAY!
AND THE CAKES DIDN'T OPEN UP SUGARCUBE CORNER THIS MORNING!
AT FIRST I THOUGHT MAYBE THEY WERE PLANNING A *PARTY* BECAUSE MR. CAKE'S BIRTHDAY IS IN 43 DAYS AND THAT'S CUTTING IT *WAY* CLOSE TO *JUST* BE STARTING IN ON ORDERING SUPPLIES...
...BUT WHEN I ASKED ABOUT IT, THEY JUST LOOKED AT ME LIKE I WAS *CRAZY.*
EVERYPONY IS ACTING SO BIZARRE! MORE AND MORE PONIES BY THE HOUR! WHAT IN EQUESTRIA IS GOING ON?
UH.... I THINK WE SHOULD MOVE THIS CONVERSATION TO SOMEWHERE MORE... PRIVATE?
QUICK GIRLS, TO THE *LIBRARY!*
THAT'S YOUR SOLUTION FOR EVERYTHING.
GALLOPING THERE MIGHT BE A GOOD IDEA.
WHAT IS *WRONG* WITH EVERYPONY?!

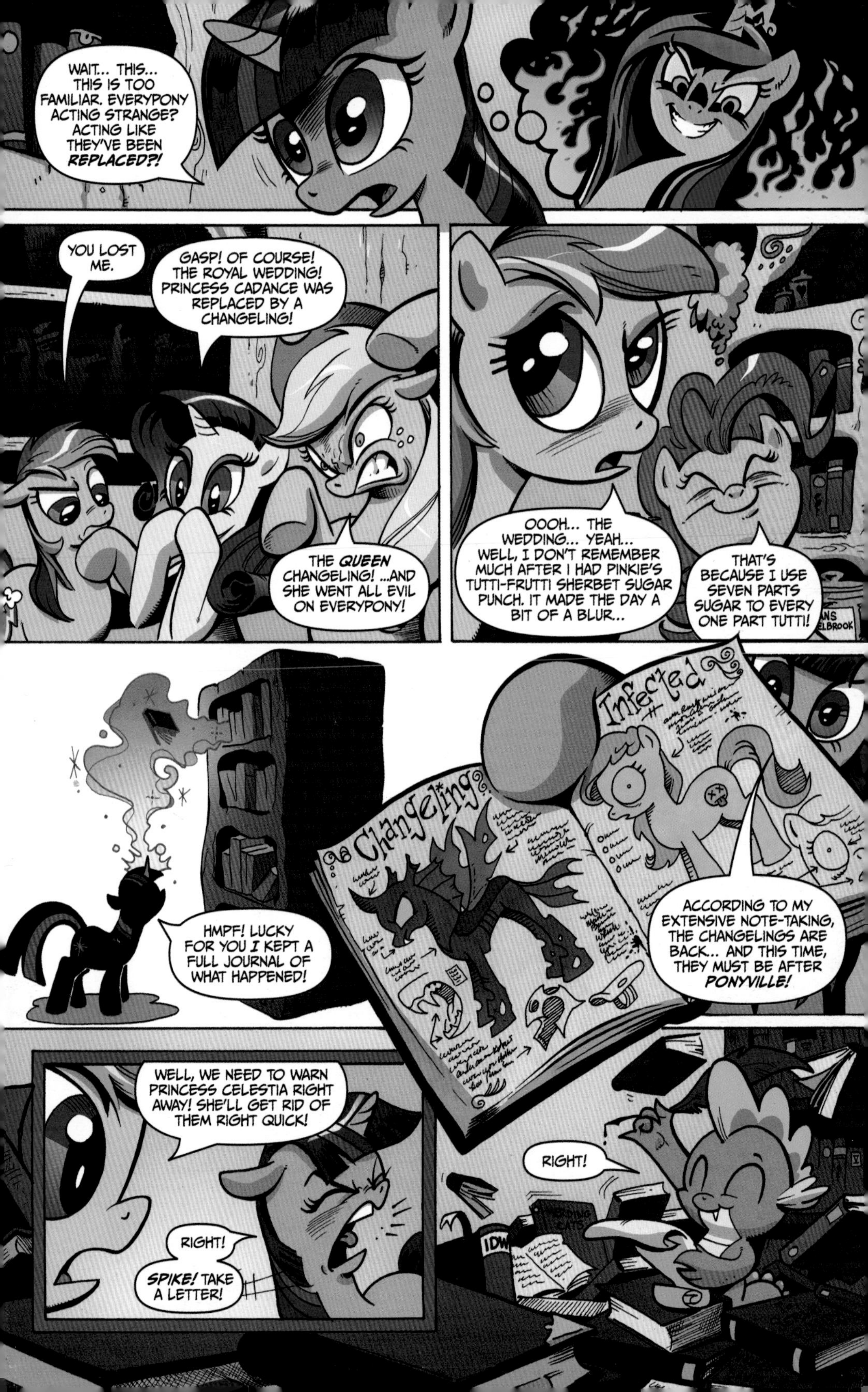

WAIT... THIS... THIS IS TOO FAMILIAR. EVERYPONY ACTING STRANGE? ACTING LIKE THEY'VE BEEN *REPLACED?!*
YOU LOST ME.
GASP! OF COURSE! THE ROYAL WEDDING! PRINCESS CADANCE WAS REPLACED BY A CHANGELING!
THE *QUEEN* CHANGELING! ...AND SHE WENT ALL EVIL ON EVERYPONY!
OOOH... THE WEDDING... YEAH... WELL, I DON'T REMEMBER MUCH AFTER I HAD PINKIE'S TUTTI-FRUTTI SHERBET SUGAR PUNCH. IT MADE THE DAY A BIT OF A BLUR...
THAT'S BECAUSE I USE SEVEN PARTS SUGAR TO EVERY ONE PART TUTTI!
HMPF! LUCKY FOR YOU *I* KEPT A FULL JOURNAL OF WHAT HAPPENED!
Changeling
Infected
ACCORDING TO MY EXTENSIVE NOTE-TAKING, THE CHANGELINGS ARE BACK... AND THIS TIME, THEY MUST BE AFTER *PONYVILLE!*
WELL, WE NEED TO WARN PRINCESS CELESTIA RIGHT AWAY! SHE'LL GET RID OF THEM RIGHT QUICK!
RIGHT!
SPIKE! TAKE A LETTER!
RIGHT!
IDW

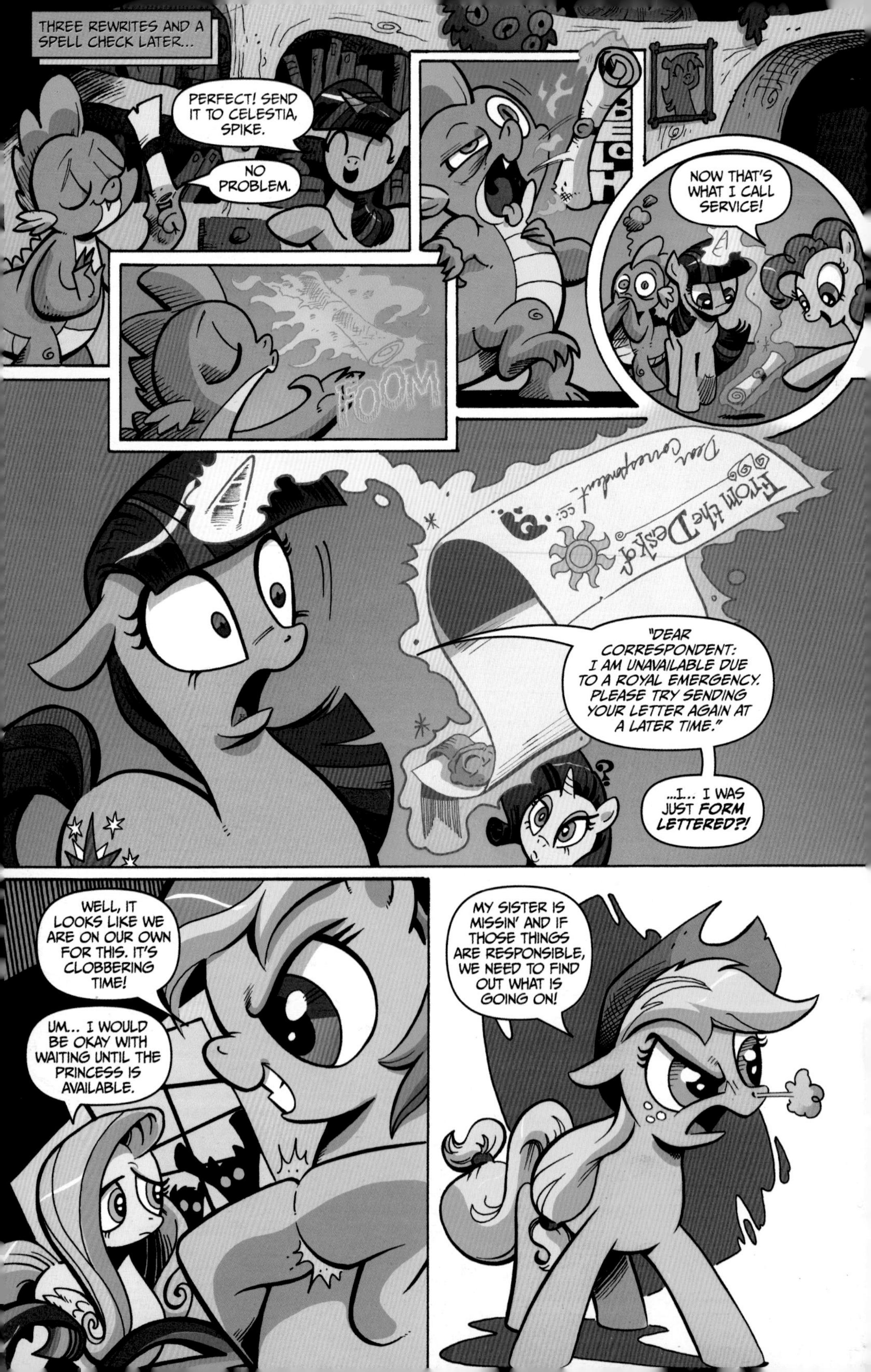
THREE REWRITES AND A SPELL CHECK LATER...
PERFECT! SEND IT TO CELESTIA, SPIKE.
NO PROBLEM.
FOOM
NOW THAT'S WHAT I CALL SERVICE!
"DEAR CORRESPONDENT: I AM UNAVAILABLE DUE TO A ROYAL EMERGENCY. PLEASE TRY SENDING YOUR LETTER AGAIN AT A LATER TIME."
...I... I WAS JUST FORM LETTERED?!
WELL, IT LOOKS LIKE WE ARE ON OUR OWN FOR THIS. IT'S CLOBBERING TIME!
UM... I WOULD BE OKAY WITH WAITING UNTIL THE PRINCESS IS AVAILABLE.
MY SISTER IS MISSIN' AND IF THOSE THINGS ARE RESPONSIBLE, WE NEED TO FIND OUT WHAT IS GOING ON!

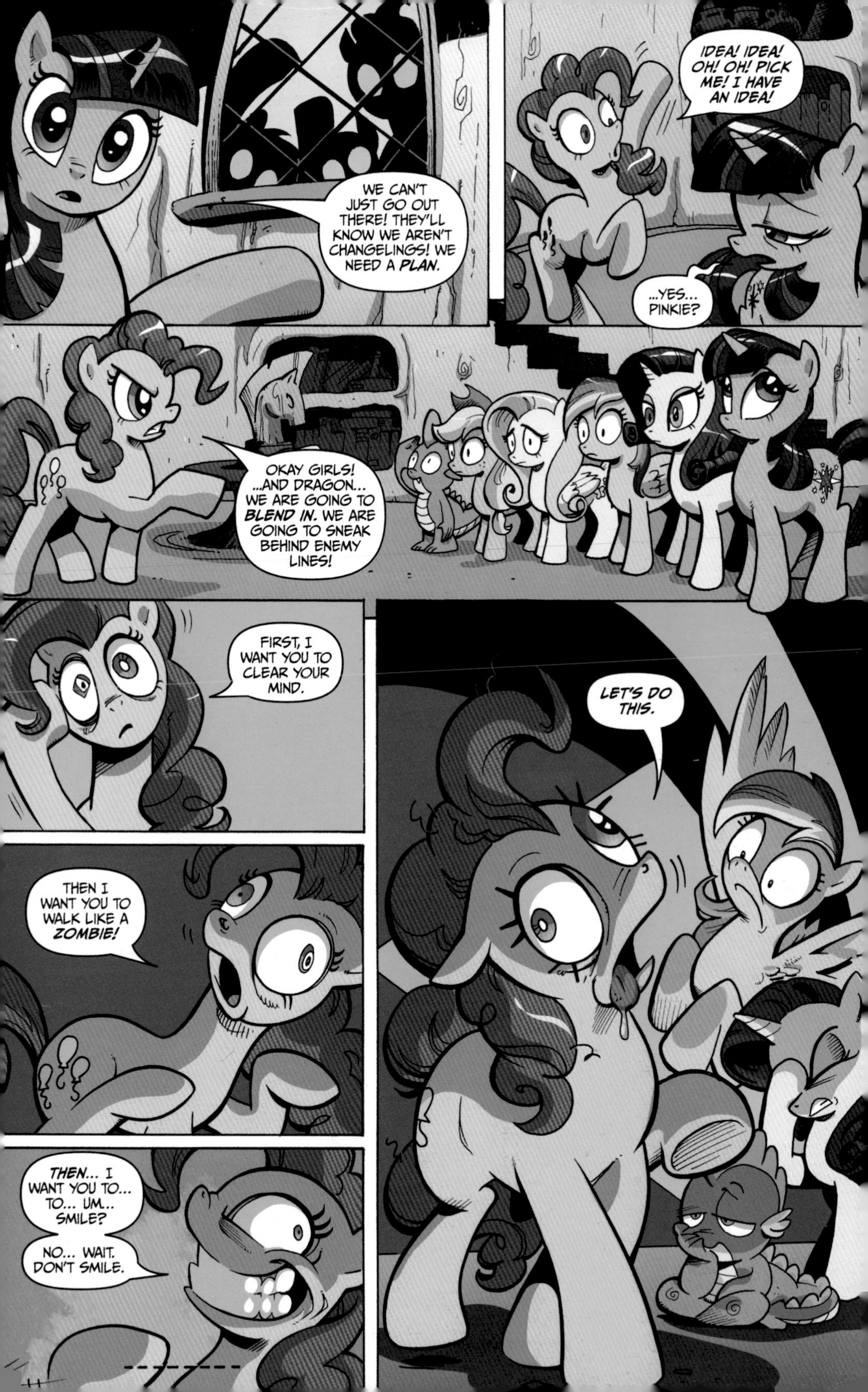
WE CAN'T JUST GO OUT THERE! THEY'LL KNOW WE AREN'T CHANGELINGS! WE NEED A PLAN.
IDEA! IDEA! OH! OH! PICK ME! I HAVE AN IDEA!
...YES... PINKIE?
OKAY GIRLS! ...AND DRAGON... WE ARE GOING TO BLEND IN. WE ARE GOING TO SNEAK BEHIND ENEMY LINES!
FIRST, I WANT YOU TO CLEAR YOUR MIND.
THEN I WANT YOU TO WALK LIKE A ZOMBIE!
THEN... I WANT YOU TO... TO... UM... SMILE?
NO... WAIT. DON'T SMILE.
LET'S DO THIS.

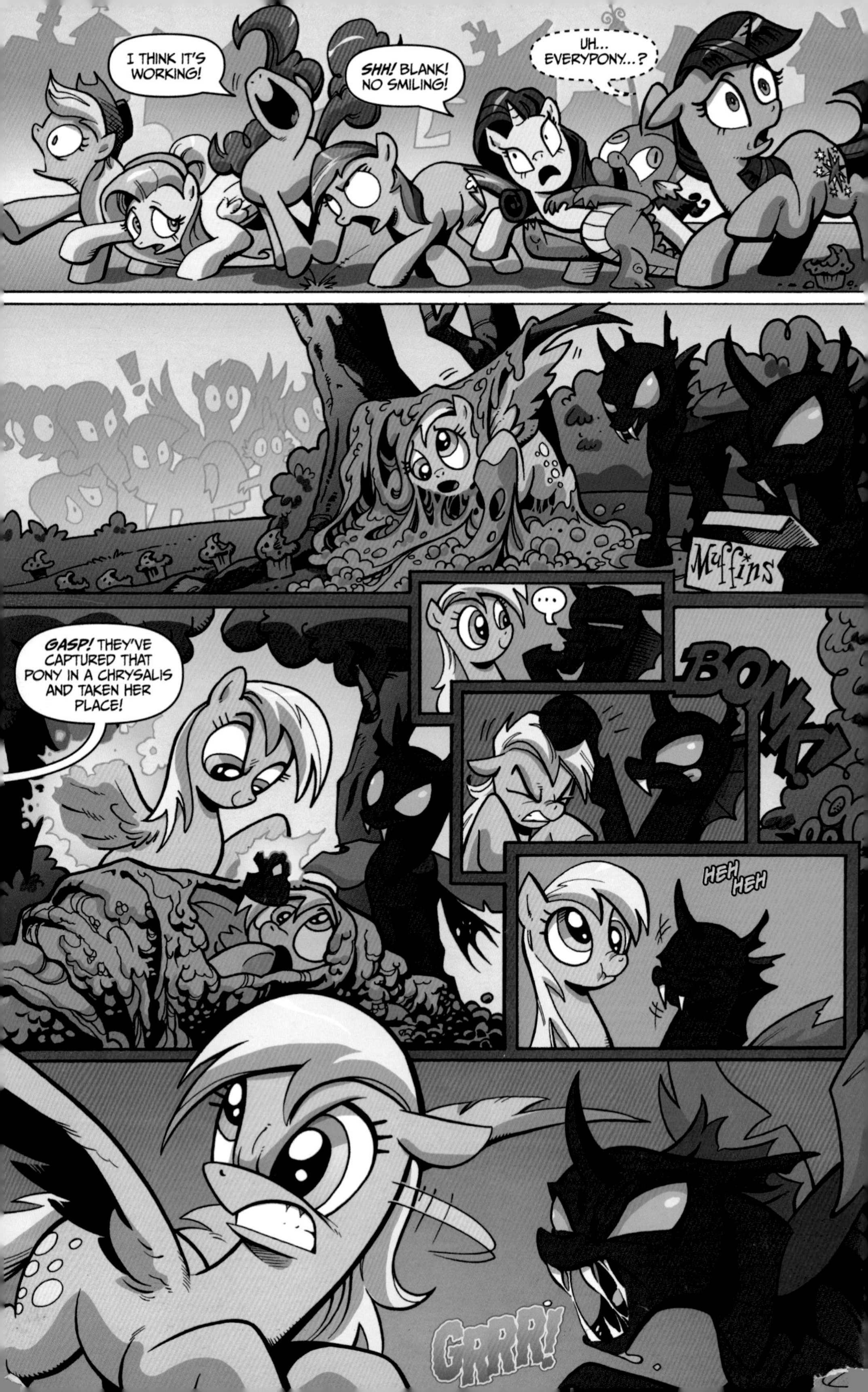
I THINK IT'S WORKING!
SHH! BLANK! NO SMILING!
UH... EVERYPONY...?
Muffins
GASP! THEY'VE CAPTURED THAT PONY IN A CHRYSALIS AND TAKEN HER PLACE!
...
BONK!
HEH HEH
GRRR!

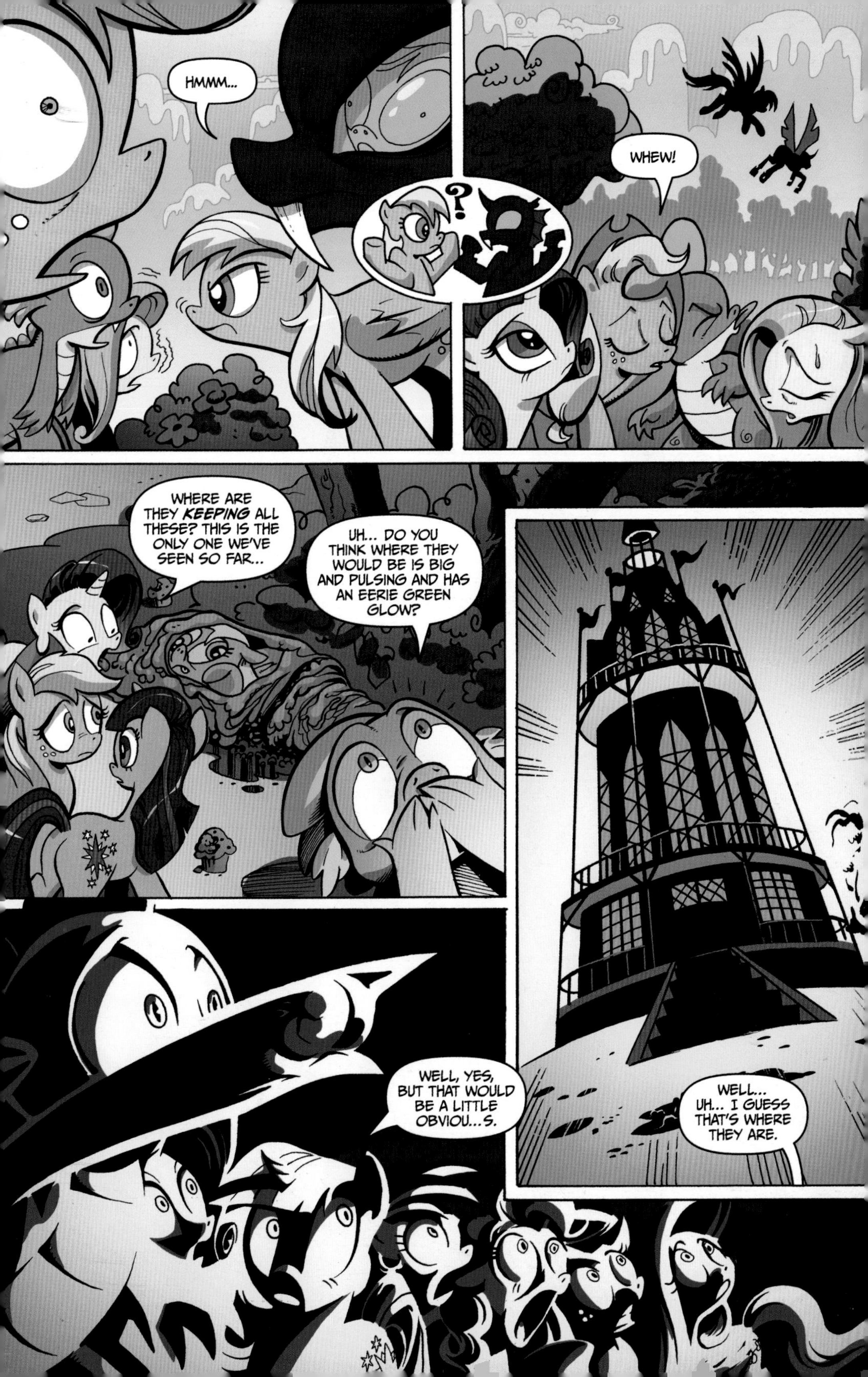
HMMM...
WHEW!
WHERE ARE THEY *KEEPING* ALL THESE? THIS IS THE ONLY ONE WE'VE SEEN SO FAR...
UH... DO YOU THINK WHERE THEY WOULD BE IS BIG AND PULSING AND HAS AN EERIE GREEN GLOW?
WELL, YES, BUT THAT WOULD BE A LITTLE OBVIOU...S.
WELL... UH... I GUESS THAT'S WHERE THEY ARE.

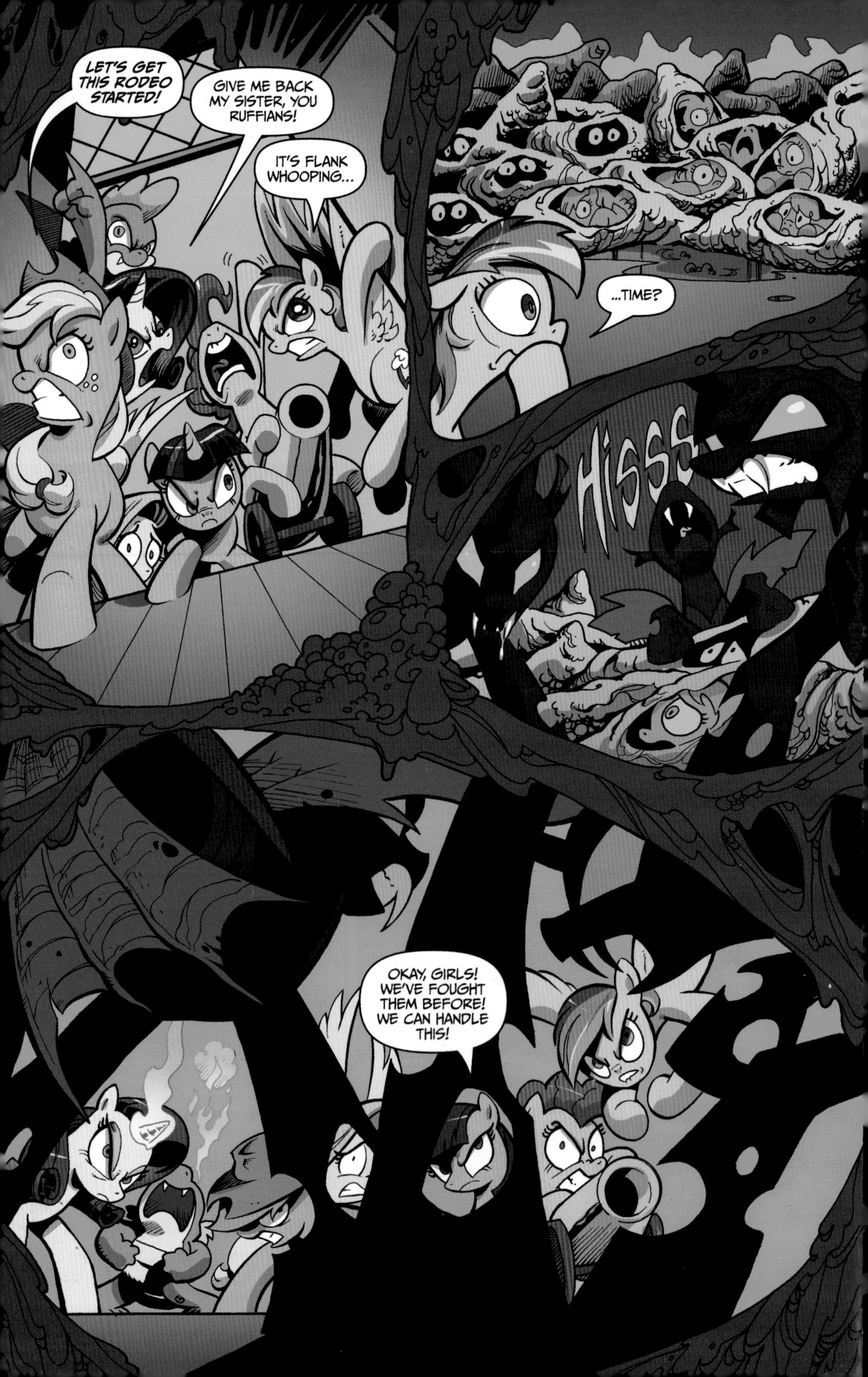
LET'S GET THIS RODEO STARTED!
GIVE ME BACK MY SISTER, YOU RUFFIANS!
IT'S FLANK WHOOPING...
...TIME?
HISSS
OKAY, GIRLS! WE'VE FOUGHT THEM BEFORE! WE CAN HANDLE THIS!

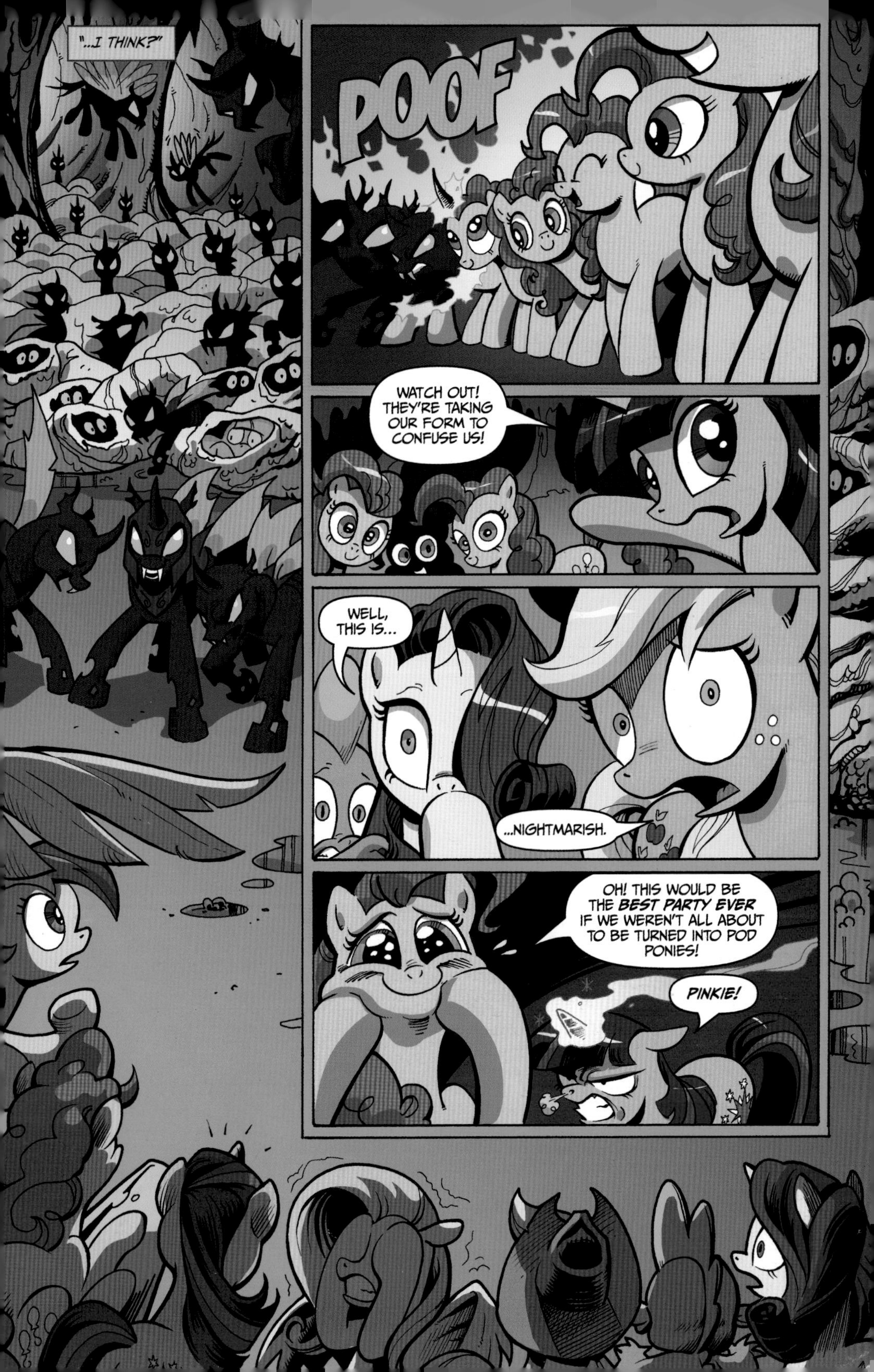
"...I THINK?"
POOF
WATCH OUT! THEY'RE TAKING OUR FORM TO CONFUSE US!
WELL, THIS IS...
...NIGHTMARISH.
OH! THIS WOULD BE THE ***BEST PARTY EVER*** IF WE WEREN'T ALL ABOUT TO BE TURNED INTO POD PONIES!
PINKIE!

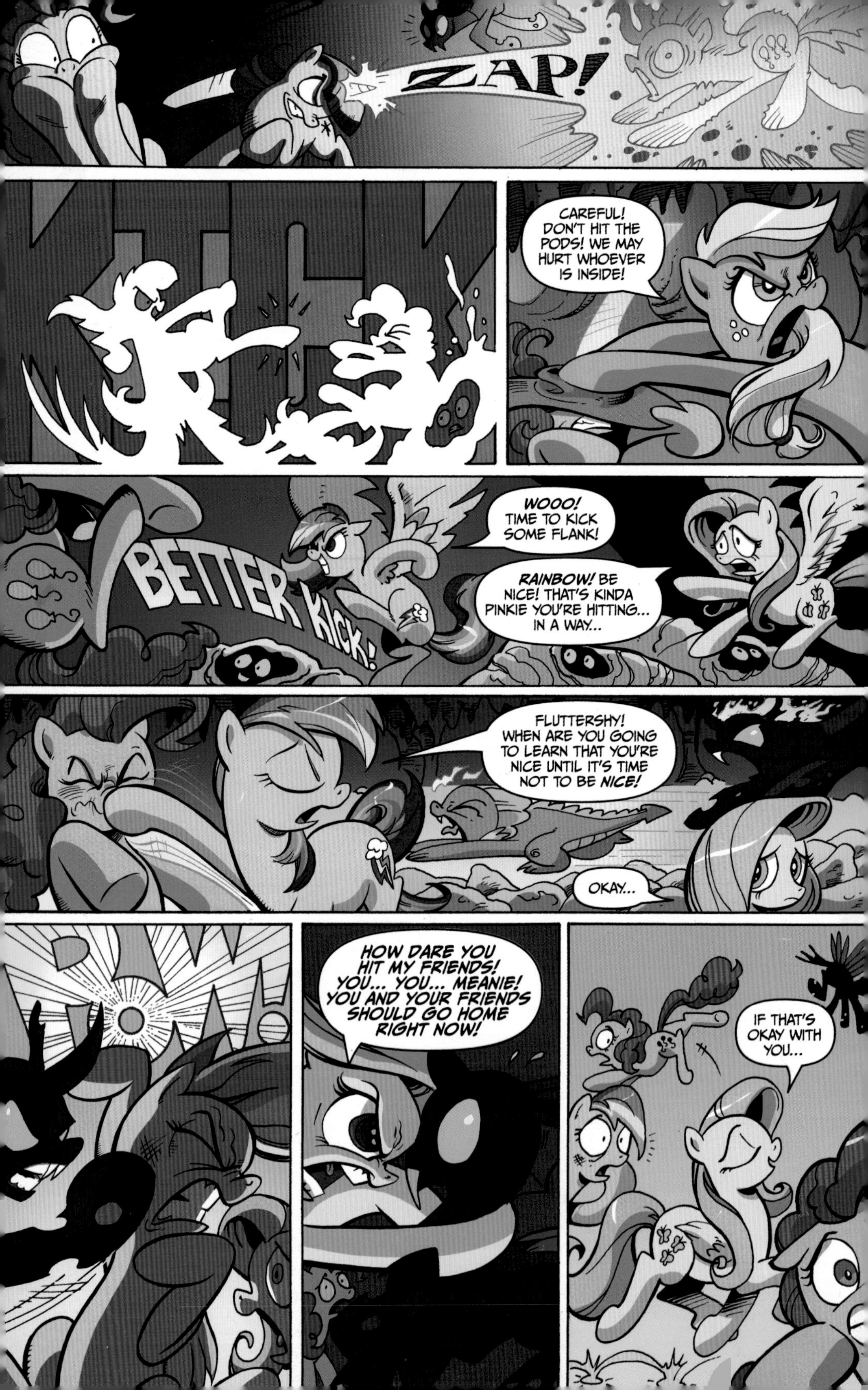
ZAP!
CAREFUL! DON'T HIT THE PODS! WE MAY HURT WHOEVER IS INSIDE!
WOOO! TIME TO KICK SOME FLANK!
BETTER KICK!
RAINBOW! BE NICE! THAT'S KINDA PINKIE YOU'RE HITTING... IN A WAY...
FLUTTERSHY! WHEN ARE YOU GOING TO LEARN THAT YOU'RE NICE UNTIL IT'S TIME NOT TO BE NICE!
OKAY...
HOW DARE YOU HIT MY FRIENDS! YOU... YOU... MEANIE! YOU AND YOUR FRIENDS SHOULD GO HOME RIGHT NOW!
IF THAT'S OKAY WITH YOU...

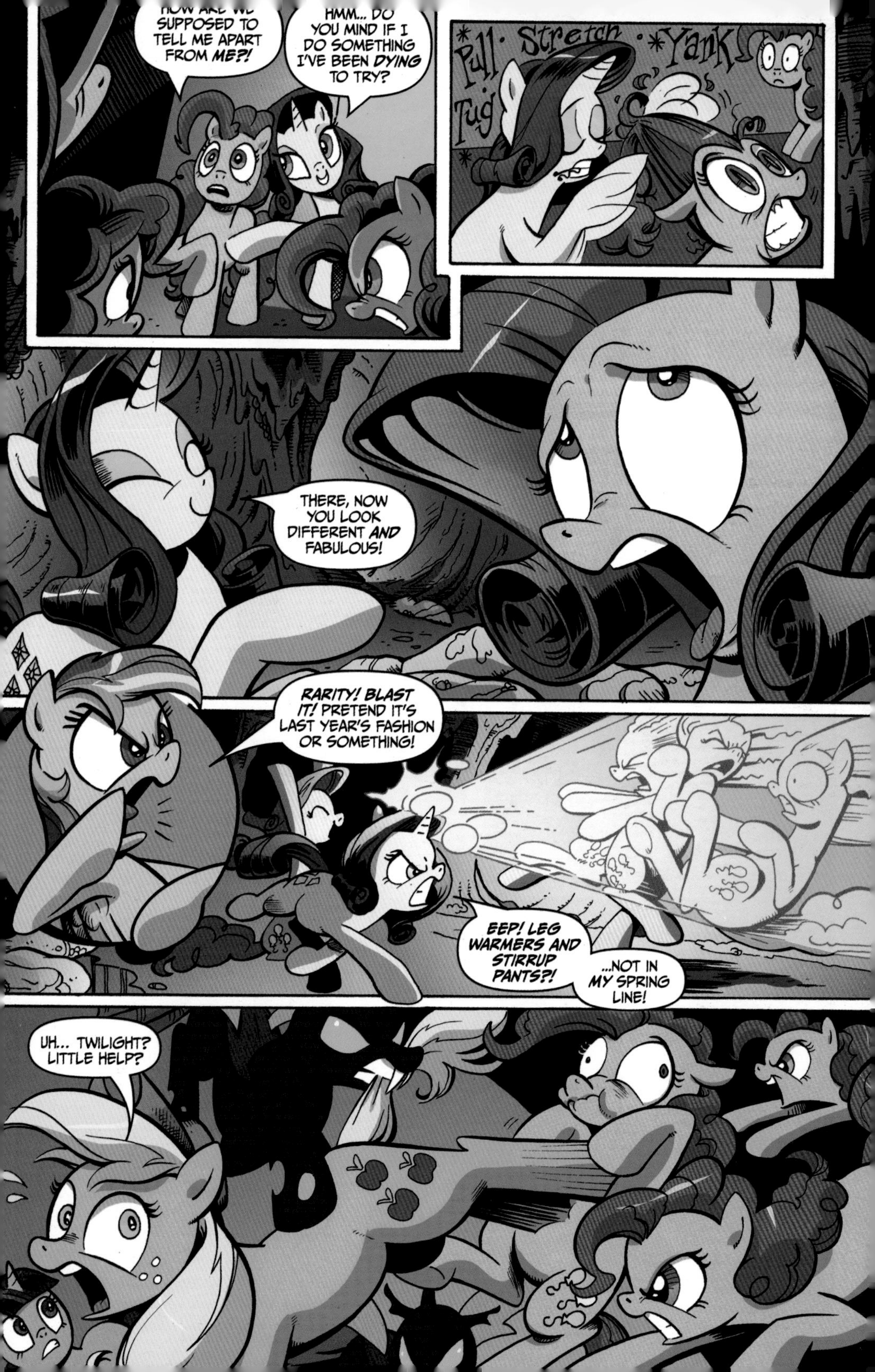
HOW ARE WE SUPPOSED TO TELL ME APART FROM ME?!
HMM... DO YOU MIND IF I DO SOMETHING I'VE BEEN DYING TO TRY?
Pull · Stretch · Yank! Tug
THERE, NOW YOU LOOK DIFFERENT AND FABULOUS!
RARITY! BLAST IT! PRETEND IT'S LAST YEAR'S FASHION OR SOMETHING!
EEP! LEG WARMERS AND STIRRUP PANTS?!
...NOT IN MY SPRING LINE!
UH... TWILIGHT? LITTLE HELP?

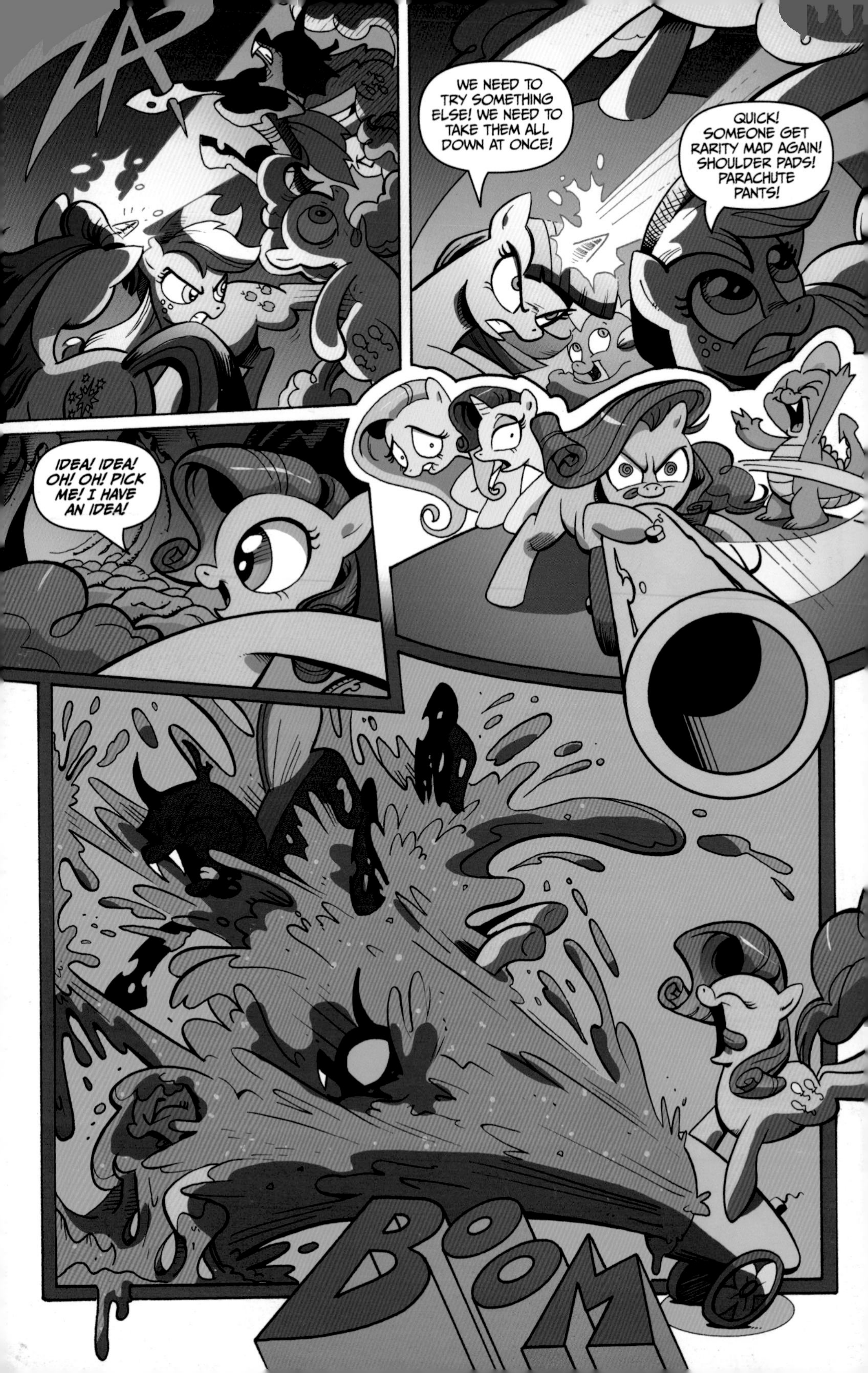
ZAP
WE NEED TO TRY SOMETHING ELSE! WE NEED TO TAKE THEM ALL DOWN AT ONCE!
QUICK! SOMEONE GET RARITY MAD AGAIN! SHOULDER PADS! PARACHUTE PANTS!
IDEA! IDEA! OH! OH! PICK ME! I HAVE AN IDEA!
BOOM

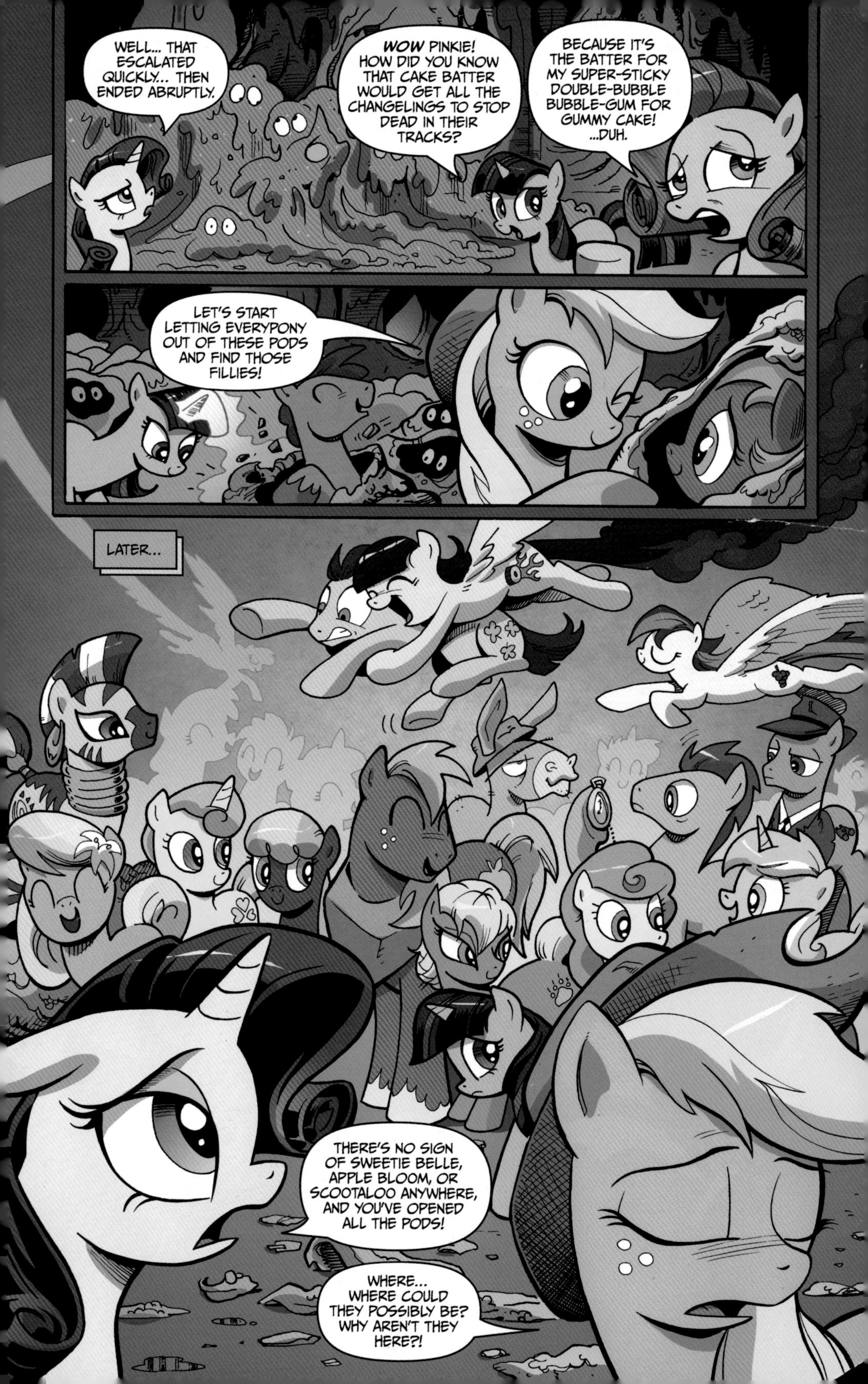
WELL... THAT ESCALATED QUICKLY... THEN ENDED ABRUPTLY.
WOW PINKIE! HOW DID YOU KNOW THAT CAKE BATTER WOULD GET ALL THE CHANGELINGS TO STOP DEAD IN THEIR TRACKS?
BECAUSE IT'S THE BATTER FOR MY SUPER-STICKY DOUBLE-BUBBLE BUBBLE-GUM FOR GUMMY CAKE! ...DUH.
LET'S START LETTING EVERYPONY OUT OF THESE PODS AND FIND THOSE FILLIES!
LATER...
THERE'S NO SIGN OF SWEETIE BELLE, APPLE BLOOM, OR SCOOTALOO ANYWHERE, AND YOU'VE OPENED ALL THE PODS!
WHERE... WHERE COULD THEY POSSIBLY BE? WHY AREN'T THEY HERE?!

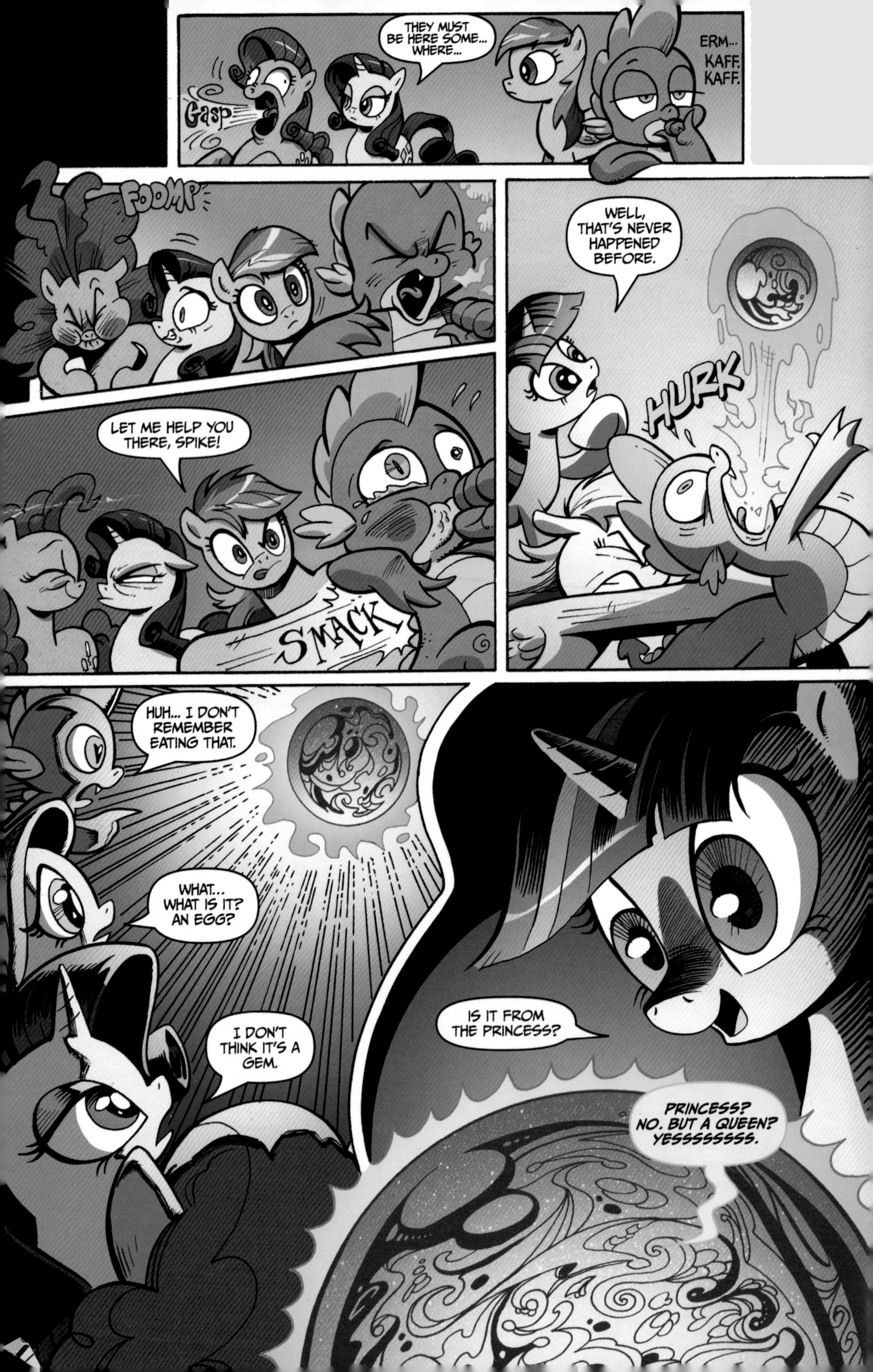
THEY MUST BE HERE SOME... WHERE...
GASP
ERM... KAFF. KAFF.
FOOMP
LET ME HELP YOU THERE, SPIKE!
SMACK
WELL, THAT'S NEVER HAPPENED BEFORE.
HURK
HUH... I DON'T REMEMBER EATING THAT.
WHAT... WHAT IS IT? AN EGG?
I DON'T THINK IT'S A GEM.
IS IT FROM THE PRINCESS?
PRINCESS? NO. BUT A QUEEN? YESSSSSSSS.

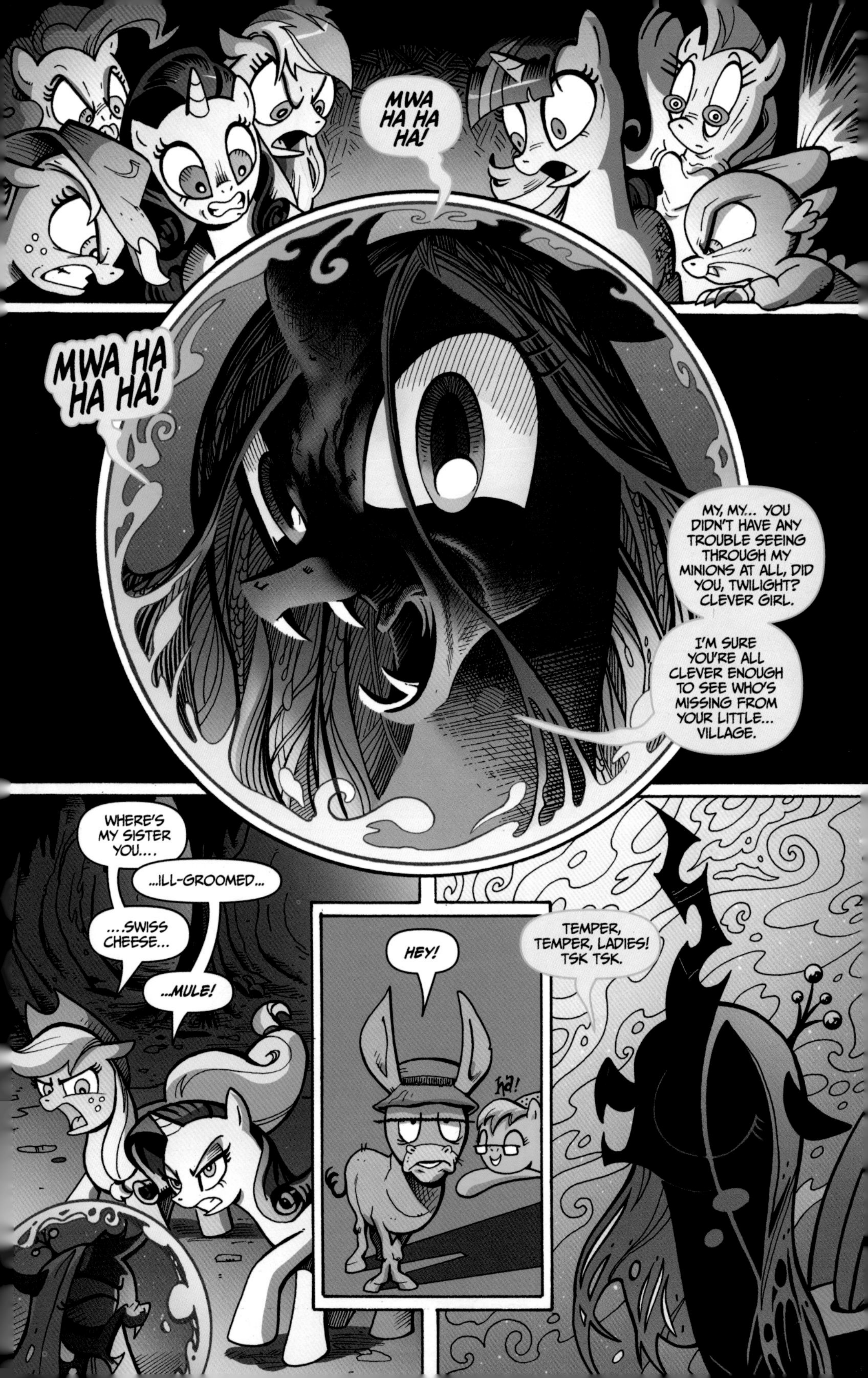
MWA HA HA HA!
MWA HA HA HA!
MY, MY... YOU DIDN'T HAVE ANY TROUBLE SEEING THROUGH MY MINIONS AT ALL, DID YOU, TWILIGHT? CLEVER GIRL.
I'M SURE YOU'RE ALL CLEVER ENOUGH TO SEE WHO'S MISSING FROM YOUR LITTLE... VILLAGE.
WHERE'S MY SISTER YOU....
...ILL-GROOMED...
....SWISS CHEESE...
...MULE!
HEY!
HA!
TEMPER, TEMPER, LADIES! TSK TSK.

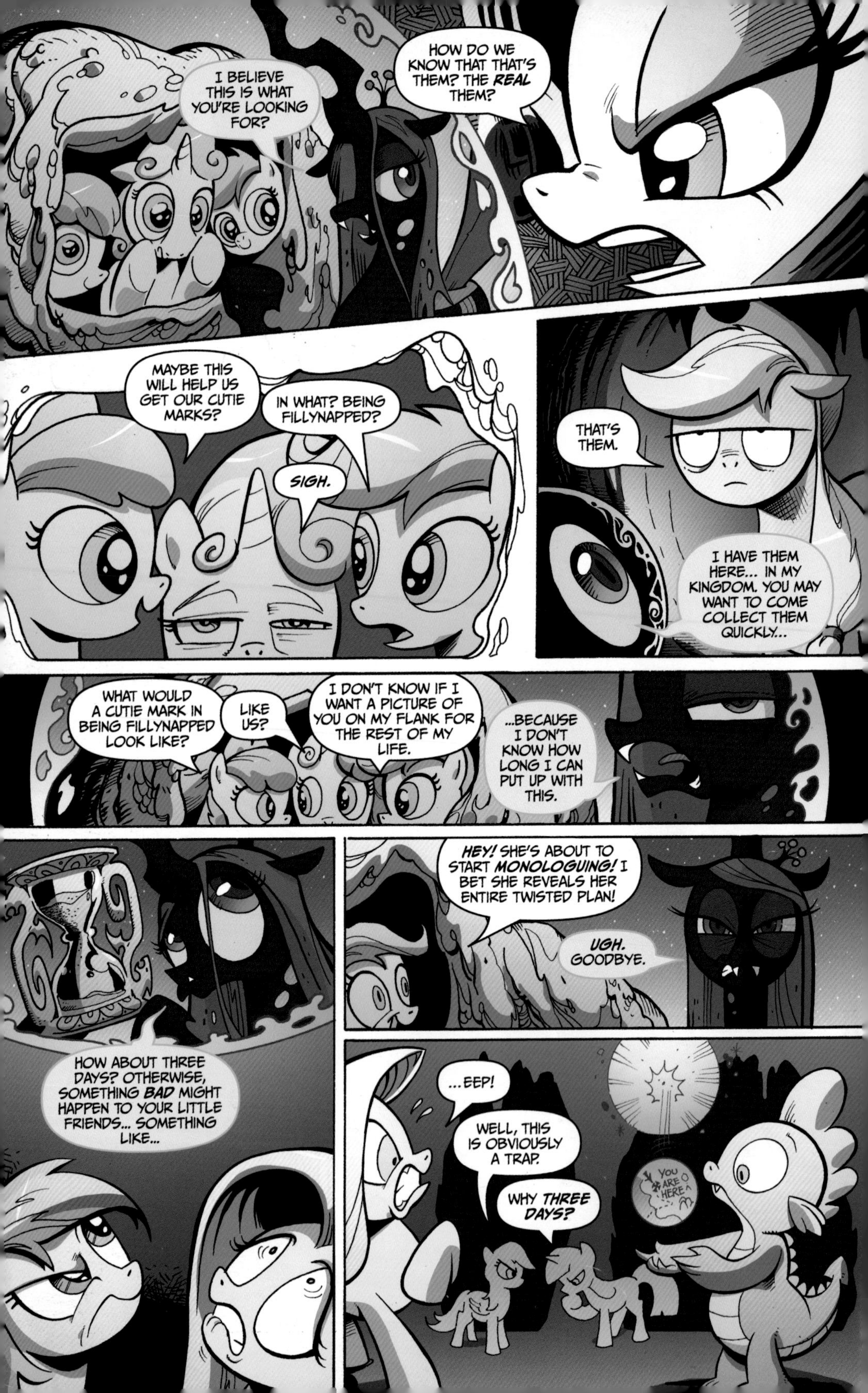
I BELIEVE THIS IS WHAT YOU'RE LOOKING FOR?
HOW DO WE KNOW THAT THAT'S THEM? THE REAL THEM?
MAYBE THIS WILL HELP US GET OUR CUTIE MARKS?
IN WHAT? BEING FILLYNAPPED?
SIGH.
THAT'S THEM.
I HAVE THEM HERE... IN MY KINGDOM. YOU MAY WANT TO COME COLLECT THEM QUICKLY...
WHAT WOULD A CUTIE MARK IN BEING FILLYNAPPED LOOK LIKE?
LIKE US?
I DON'T KNOW IF I WANT A PICTURE OF YOU ON MY FLANK FOR THE REST OF MY LIFE.
...BECAUSE I DON'T KNOW HOW LONG I CAN PUT UP WITH THIS.
HOW ABOUT THREE DAYS? OTHERWISE, SOMETHING BAD MIGHT HAPPEN TO YOUR LITTLE FRIENDS... SOMETHING LIKE...
HEY! SHE'S ABOUT TO START MONOLOGUING! I BET SHE REVEALS HER ENTIRE TWISTED PLAN!
UGH. GOODBYE.
...EEP!
WELL, THIS IS OBVIOUSLY A TRAP.
WHY THREE DAYS?
YOU ARE HERE

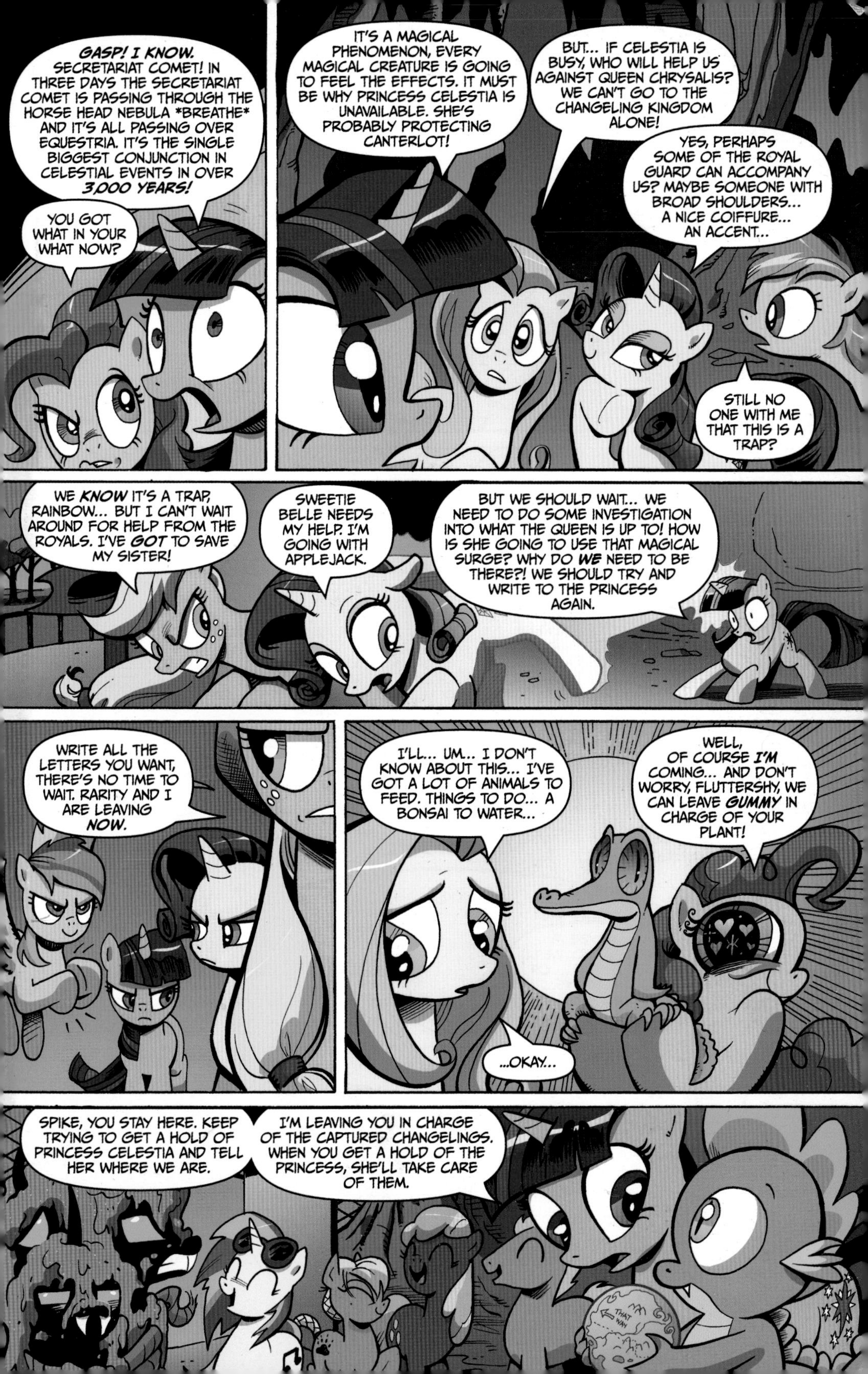
GASP! I KNOW. SECRETARIAT COMET! IN THREE DAYS THE SECRETARIAT COMET IS PASSING THROUGH THE HORSE HEAD NEBULA *BREATHE* AND IT'S ALL PASSING OVER EQUESTRIA. IT'S THE SINGLE BIGGEST CONJUNCTION IN CELESTIAL EVENTS IN OVER 3,000 YEARS!
YOU GOT WHAT IN YOUR WHAT NOW?
IT'S A MAGICAL PHENOMENON, EVERY MAGICAL CREATURE IS GOING TO FEEL THE EFFECTS. IT MUST BE WHY PRINCESS CELESTIA IS UNAVAILABLE. SHE'S PROBABLY PROTECTING CANTERLOT!
BUT... IF CELESTIA IS BUSY, WHO WILL HELP US AGAINST QUEEN CHRYSALIS? WE CAN'T GO TO THE CHANGELING KINGDOM ALONE!
YES, PERHAPS SOME OF THE ROYAL GUARD CAN ACCOMPANY US? MAYBE SOMEONE WITH BROAD SHOULDERS... A NICE COIFFURE... AN ACCENT...
STILL NO ONE WITH ME THAT THIS IS A TRAP?
WE KNOW IT'S A TRAP, RAINBOW... BUT I CAN'T WAIT AROUND FOR HELP FROM THE ROYALS. I'VE GOT TO SAVE MY SISTER!
SWEETIE BELLE NEEDS MY HELP. I'M GOING WITH APPLEJACK.
BUT WE SHOULD WAIT... WE NEED TO DO SOME INVESTIGATION INTO WHAT THE QUEEN IS UP TO! HOW IS SHE GOING TO USE THAT MAGICAL SURGE? WHY DO WE NEED TO BE THERE?! WE SHOULD TRY AND WRITE TO THE PRINCESS AGAIN.
WRITE ALL THE LETTERS YOU WANT, THERE'S NO TIME TO WAIT. RARITY AND I ARE LEAVING NOW.
I'LL... UM... I DON'T KNOW ABOUT THIS... I'VE GOT A LOT OF ANIMALS TO FEED. THINGS TO DO... A BONSAI TO WATER...
WELL, OF COURSE I'M COMING... AND DON'T WORRY, FLUTTERSHY, WE CAN LEAVE GUMMY IN CHARGE OF YOUR PLANT!
...OKAY...
SPIKE, YOU STAY HERE. KEEP TRYING TO GET A HOLD OF PRINCESS CELESTIA AND TELL HER WHERE WE ARE.
I'M LEAVING YOU IN CHARGE OF THE CAPTURED CHANGELINGS. WHEN YOU GET A HOLD OF THE PRINCESS, SHE'LL TAKE CARE OF THEM.
THAT WAY

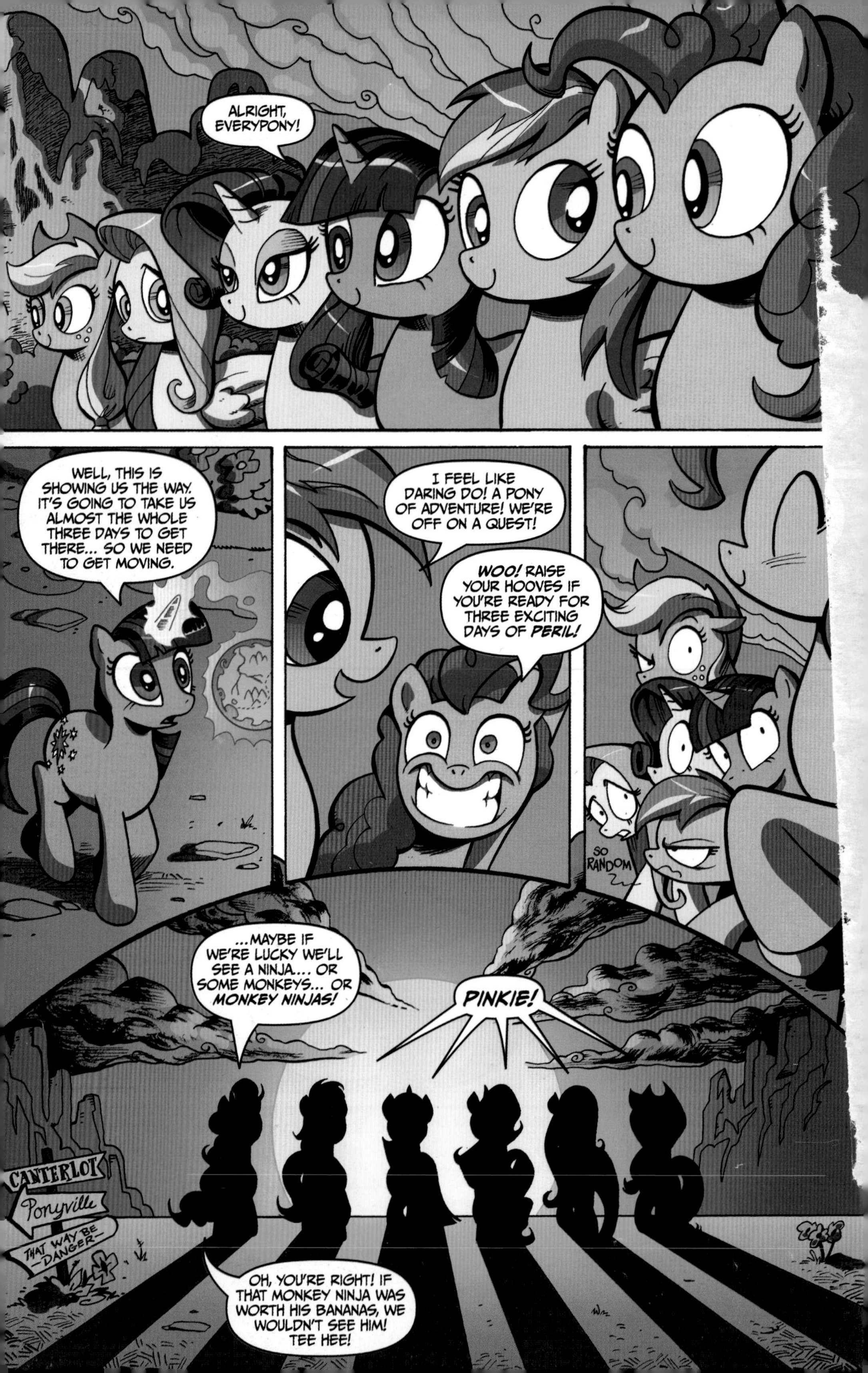
ALRIGHT, EVERYPONY!
WELL, THIS IS SHOWING US THE WAY. IT'S GOING TO TAKE US ALMOST THE WHOLE THREE DAYS TO GET THERE... SO WE NEED TO GET MOVING.
I FEEL LIKE DARING DO! A PONY OF ADVENTURE! WE'RE OFF ON A QUEST!
WOO! RAISE YOUR HOOVES IF YOU'RE READY FOR THREE EXCITING DAYS OF PERIL!
SO RANDOM
...MAYBE IF WE'RE LUCKY WE'LL SEE A NINJA... OR SOME MONKEYS... OR MONKEY NINJAS!
PINKIE!
CANTERLOT
Ponyville
THAT WAY BE -DANGER-
OH, YOU'RE RIGHT! IF THAT MONKEY NINJA WAS WORTH HIS BANANAS, WE WOULDN'T SEE HIM! TEE HEE!

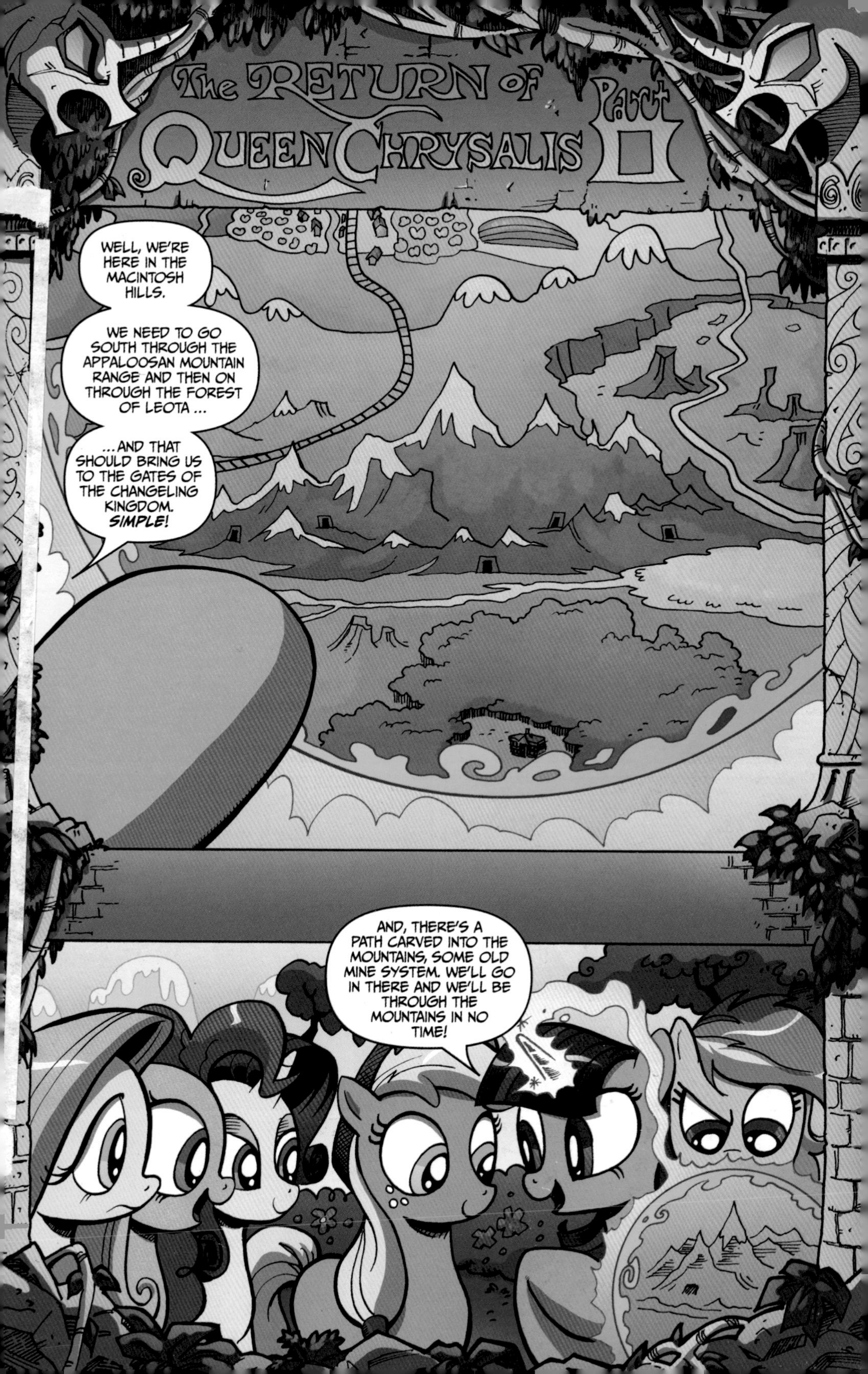
The RETURN of QUEEN CHRYSALIS Part II
WELL, WE'RE HERE IN THE MACINTOSH HILLS.
WE NEED TO GO SOUTH THROUGH THE APPALOOSAN MOUNTAIN RANGE AND THEN ON THROUGH THE FOREST OF LEOTA ...
...AND THAT SHOULD BRING US TO THE GATES OF THE CHANGELING KINGDOM. SIMPLE!
AND, THERE'S A PATH CARVED INTO THE MOUNTAINS, SOME OLD MINE SYSTEM. WE'LL GO IN THERE AND WE'LL BE THROUGH THE MOUNTAINS IN NO TIME!

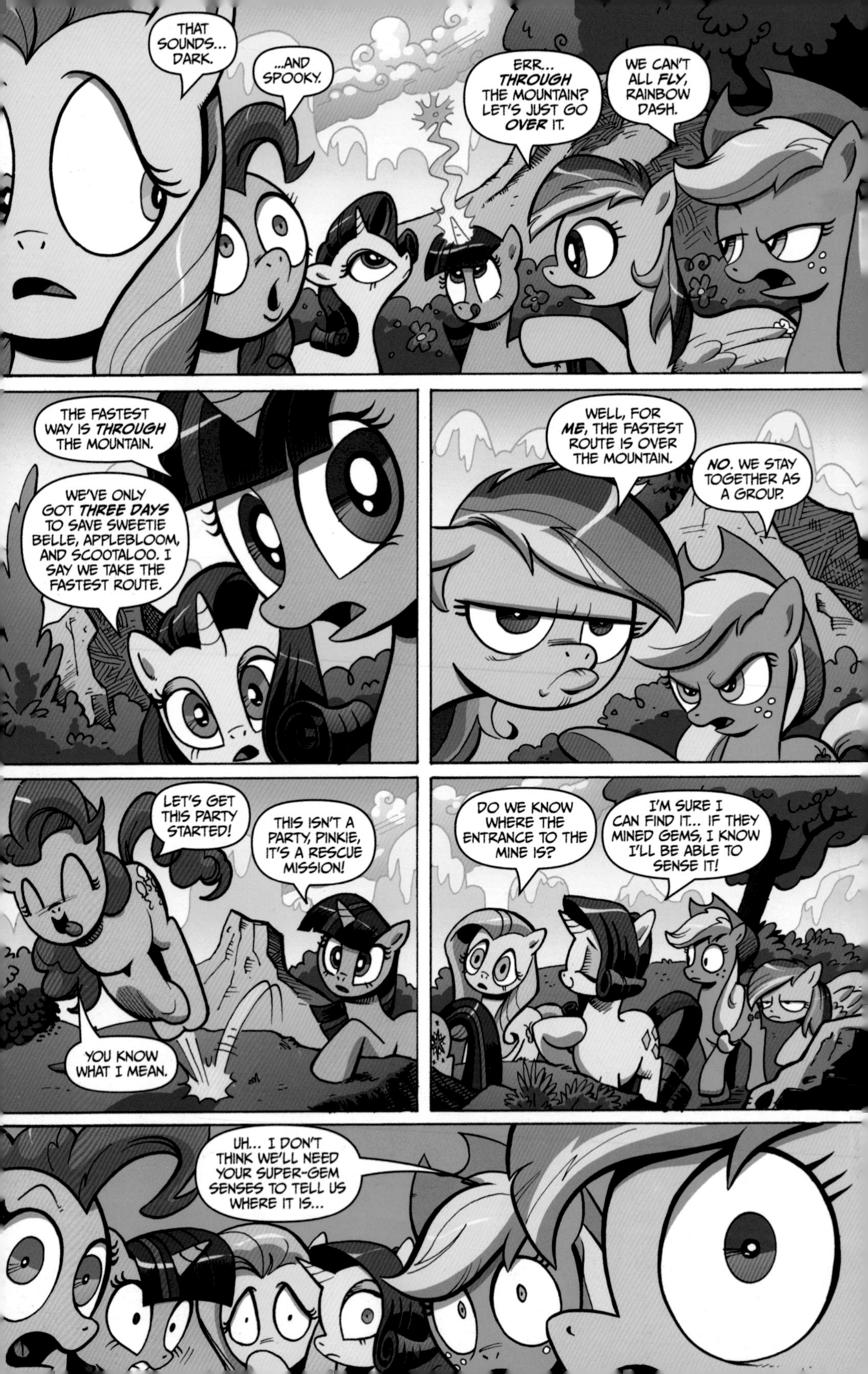

THAT SOUNDS... DARK.
...AND SPOOKY.
ERR... THROUGH THE MOUNTAIN? LET'S JUST GO OVER IT.
WE CAN'T ALL FLY, RAINBOW DASH.
THE FASTEST WAY IS THROUGH THE MOUNTAIN.
WE'VE ONLY GOT THREE DAYS TO SAVE SWEETIE BELLE, APPLEBLOOM, AND SCOOTALOO. I SAY WE TAKE THE FASTEST ROUTE.
WELL, FOR ME, THE FASTEST ROUTE IS OVER THE MOUNTAIN.
NO. WE STAY TOGETHER AS A GROUP.
LET'S GET THIS PARTY STARTED!
THIS ISN'T A PARTY, PINKIE, IT'S A RESCUE MISSION!
YOU KNOW WHAT I MEAN.
DO WE KNOW WHERE THE ENTRANCE TO THE MINE IS?
I'M SURE I CAN FIND IT... IF THEY MINED GEMS, I KNOW I'LL BE ABLE TO SENSE IT!
UH... I DON'T THINK WE'LL NEED YOUR SUPER-GEM SENSES TO TELL US WHERE IT IS...

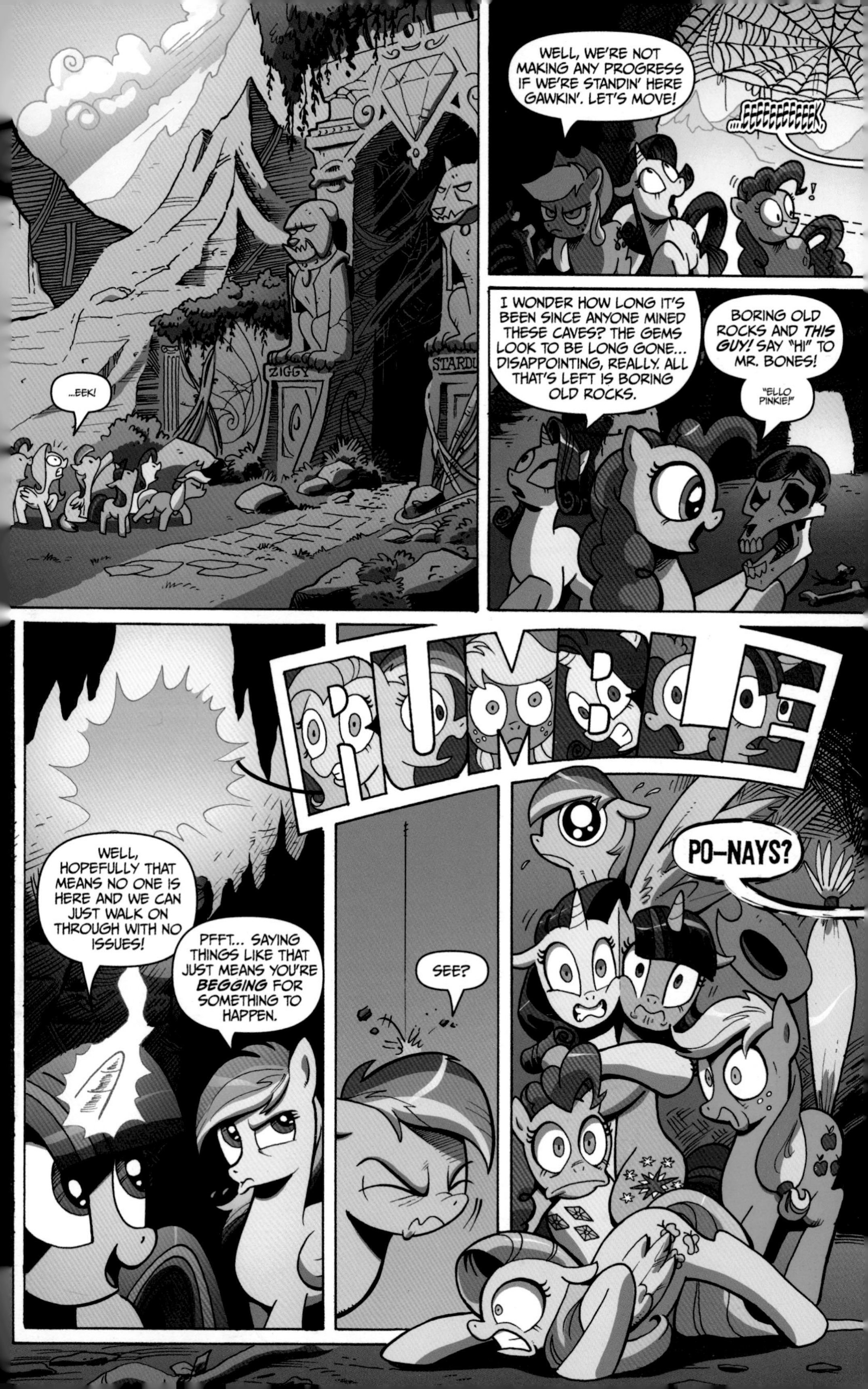
ZIGGY
STARDU
...EEK!
WELL, WE'RE NOT MAKING ANY PROGRESS IF WE'RE STANDIN' HERE GAWKIN'. LET'S MOVE!
...EEEEEEEEEEEK.
!
I WONDER HOW LONG IT'S BEEN SINCE ANYONE MINED THESE CAVES? THE GEMS LOOK TO BE LONG GONE... DISAPPOINTING, REALLY. ALL THAT'S LEFT IS BORING OLD ROCKS.
BORING OLD ROCKS AND THIS GUY! SAY "HI" TO MR. BONES!
"ELLO PINKIE!"
WELL, HOPEFULLY THAT MEANS NO ONE IS HERE AND WE CAN JUST WALK ON THROUGH WITH NO ISSUES!
PFFT... SAYING THINGS LIKE THAT JUST MEANS YOU'RE BEGGING FOR SOMETHING TO HAPPEN.
SEE?
RUMBLE
PO-NAYS?

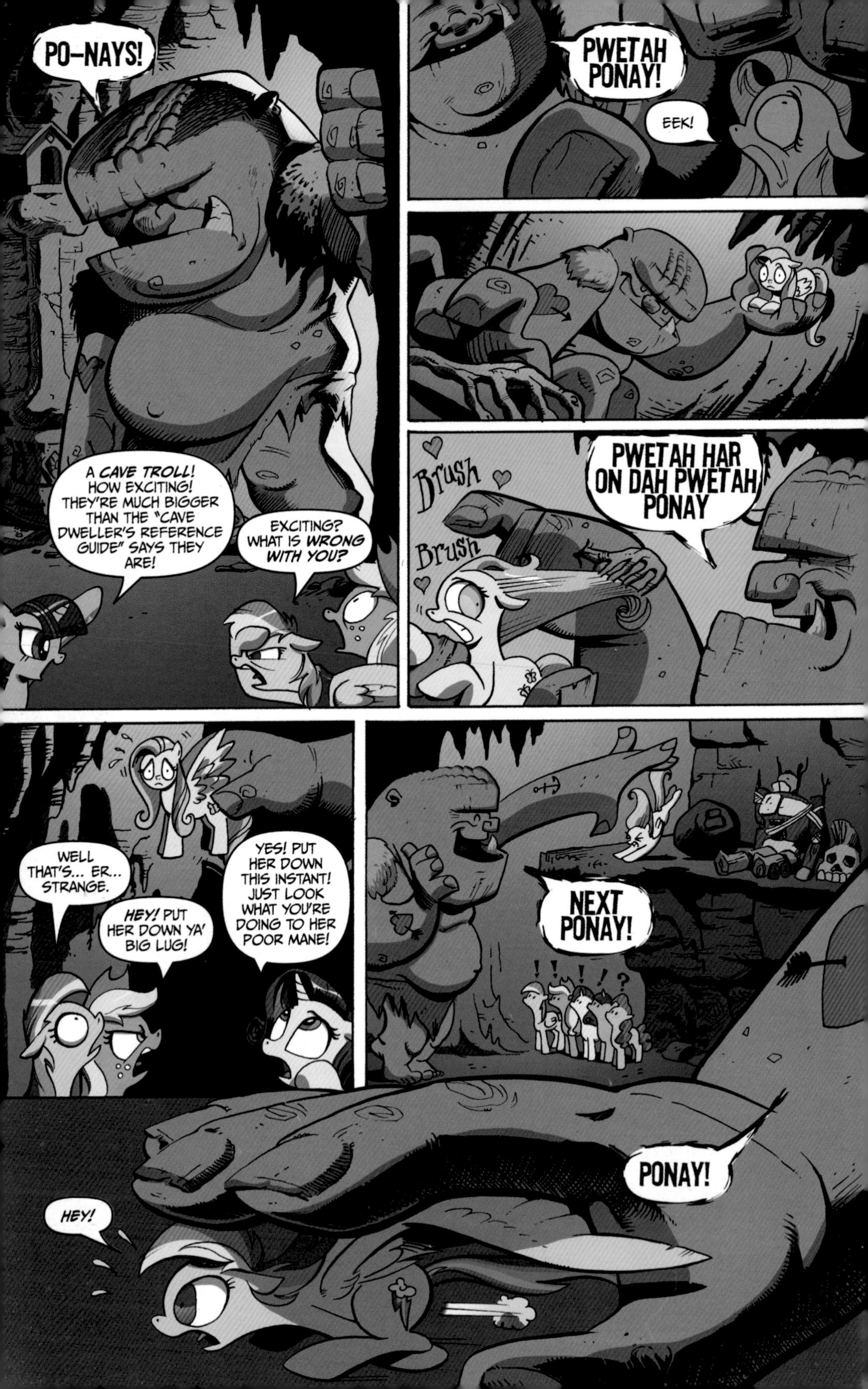
PO-NAYS!
A CAVE TROLL! HOW EXCITING! THEY'RE MUCH BIGGER THAN THE "CAVE DWELLER'S REFERENCE GUIDE" SAYS THEY ARE!
EXCITING? WHAT IS WRONG WITH YOU?
PWETAH PONAY!
EEK!
Brush
Brush
PWETAH HAR ON DAH PWETAH PONAY
WELL THAT'S... ER... STRANGE.
HEY! PUT HER DOWN YA' BIG LUG!
YES! PUT HER DOWN THIS INSTANT! JUST LOOK WHAT YOU'RE DOING TO HER POOR MANE!
NEXT PONAY!
! ! ! ! ?
PONAY!
HEY!

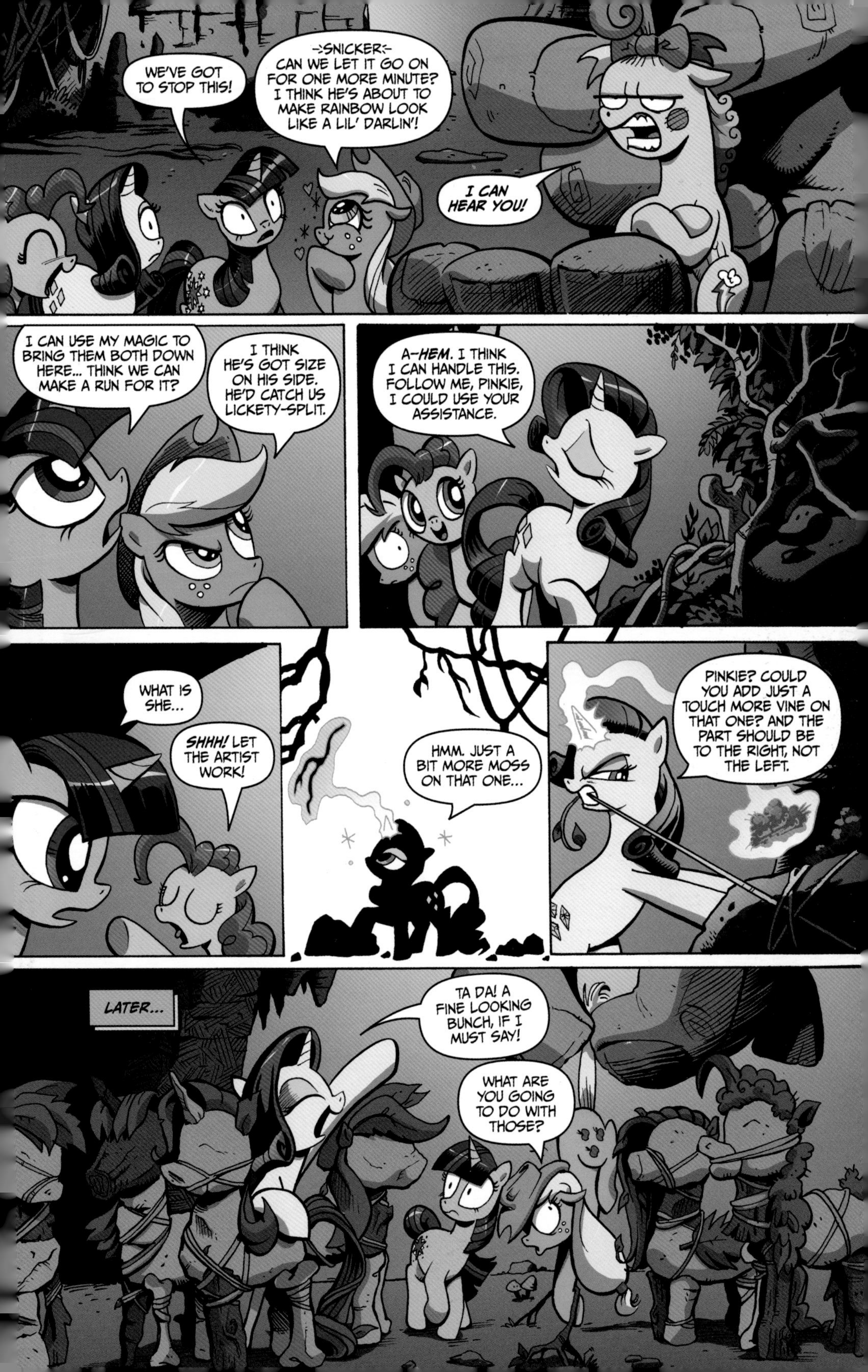

WE'VE GOT TO STOP THIS!
-SNICKER- CAN WE LET IT GO ON FOR ONE MORE MINUTE? I THINK HE'S ABOUT TO MAKE RAINBOW LOOK LIKE A LIL' DARLIN'!
I CAN HEAR YOU!
I CAN USE MY MAGIC TO BRING THEM BOTH DOWN HERE... THINK WE CAN MAKE A RUN FOR IT?
I THINK HE'S GOT SIZE ON HIS SIDE. HE'D CATCH US LICKETY-SPLIT.
A-HEM. I THINK I CAN HANDLE THIS. FOLLOW ME, PINKIE, I COULD USE YOUR ASSISTANCE.
WHAT IS SHE...
SHHH! LET THE ARTIST WORK!
HMM. JUST A BIT MORE MOSS ON THAT ONE...
PINKIE? COULD YOU ADD JUST A TOUCH MORE VINE ON THAT ONE? AND THE PART SHOULD BE TO THE RIGHT, NOT THE LEFT.
LATER...
TA DA! A FINE LOOKING BUNCH, IF I MUST SAY!
WHAT ARE YOU GOING TO DO WITH THOSE?

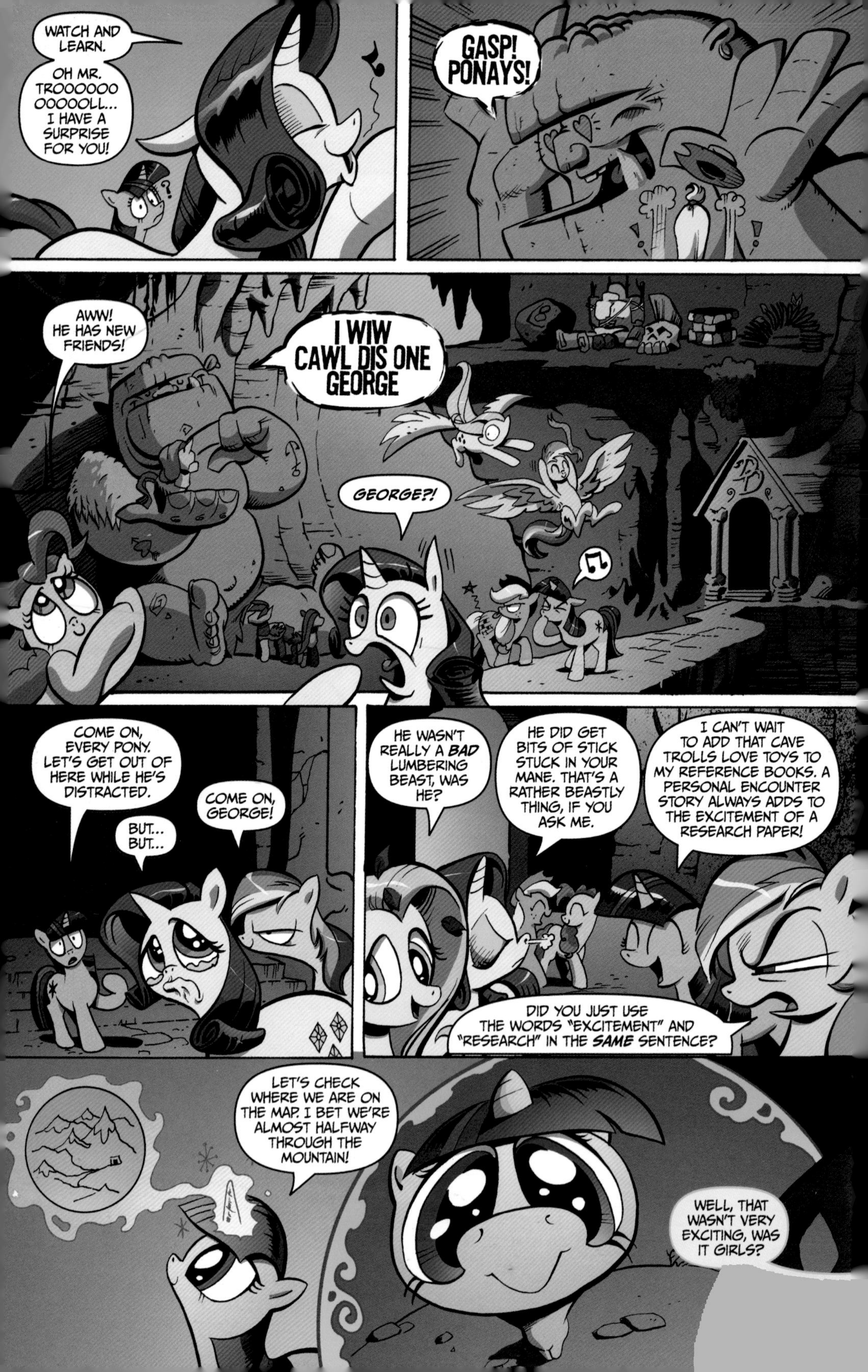
WATCH AND LEARN.
OH MR. TROOOOOO OOOOOLL... I HAVE A SURPRISE FOR YOU!
GASP! PONAYS!
AWW! HE HAS NEW FRIENDS!
I WIW CAWL DIS ONE GEORGE
GEORGE?!
COME ON, EVERY PONY. LET'S GET OUT OF HERE WHILE HE'S DISTRACTED.
BUT... BUT...
COME ON, GEORGE!
HE WASN'T REALLY A BAD LUMBERING BEAST, WAS HE?
HE DID GET BITS OF STICK STUCK IN YOUR MANE. THAT'S A RATHER BEASTLY THING, IF YOU ASK ME.
I CAN'T WAIT TO ADD THAT CAVE TROLLS LOVE TOYS TO MY REFERENCE BOOKS. A PERSONAL ENCOUNTER STORY ALWAYS ADDS TO THE EXCITEMENT OF A RESEARCH PAPER!
DID YOU JUST USE THE WORDS "EXCITEMENT" AND "RESEARCH" IN THE SAME SENTENCE?
LET'S CHECK WHERE WE ARE ON THE MAP. I BET WE'RE ALMOST HALFWAY THROUGH THE MOUNTAIN!
WELL, THAT WASN'T VERY EXCITING, WAS IT GIRLS?

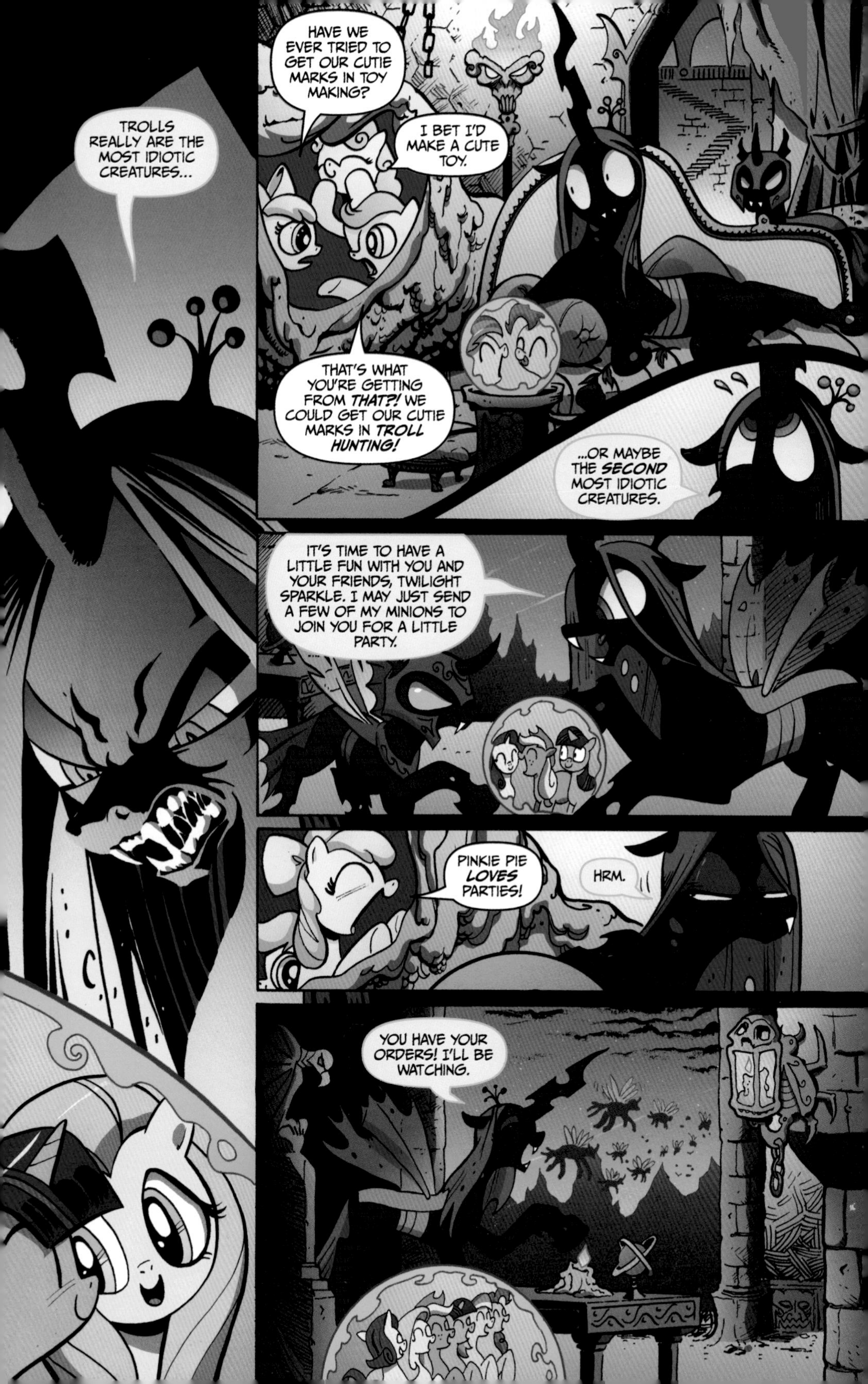
TROLLS REALLY ARE THE MOST IDIOTIC CREATURES...
HAVE WE EVER TRIED TO GET OUR CUTIE MARKS IN TOY MAKING?
I BET I'D MAKE A CUTE TOY.
THAT'S WHAT YOU'RE GETTING FROM *THAT?!* WE COULD GET OUR CUTIE MARKS IN *TROLL HUNTING!*
...OR MAYBE THE *SECOND* MOST IDIOTIC CREATURES.
IT'S TIME TO HAVE A LITTLE FUN WITH YOU AND YOUR FRIENDS, TWILIGHT SPARKLE. I MAY JUST SEND A FEW OF MY MINIONS TO JOIN YOU FOR A LITTLE PARTY.
PINKIE PIE *LOVES* PARTIES!
HRM.
YOU HAVE YOUR ORDERS! I'LL BE WATCHING.

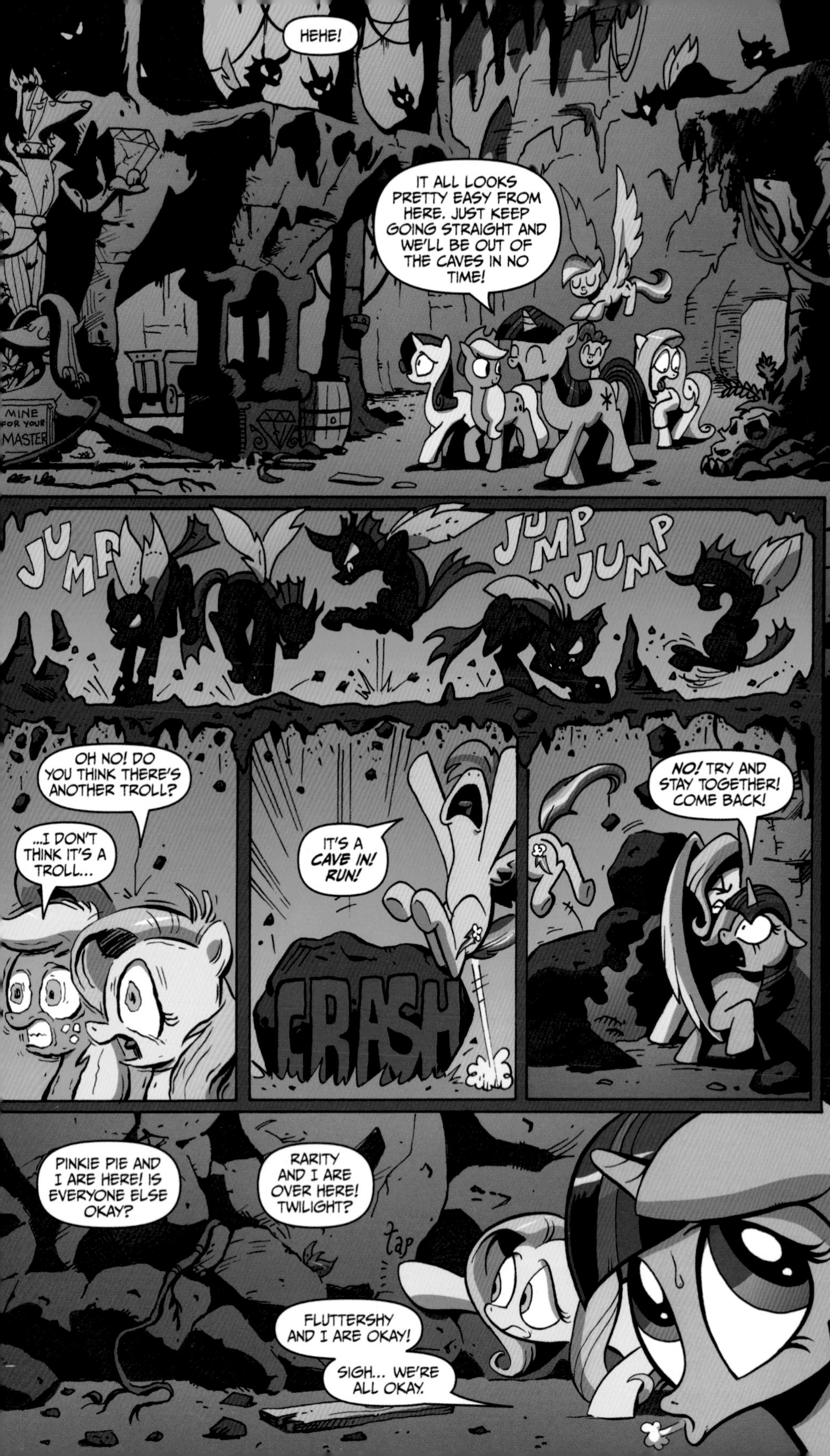
HEHE!
IT ALL LOOKS PRETTY EASY FROM HERE. JUST KEEP GOING STRAIGHT AND WE'LL BE OUT OF THE CAVES IN NO TIME!
MINE FOR YOUR MASTER
JUMP
JUMP
JUMP
OH NO! DO YOU THINK THERE'S ANOTHER TROLL?
...I DON'T THINK IT'S A TROLL...
IT'S A CAVE IN! RUN!
CRASH
NO! TRY AND STAY TOGETHER! COME BACK!
PINKIE PIE AND I ARE HERE! IS EVERYONE ELSE OKAY?
RARITY AND I ARE OVER HERE! TWILIGHT?
tap
FLUTTERSHY AND I ARE OKAY!
SIGH... WE'RE ALL OKAY.

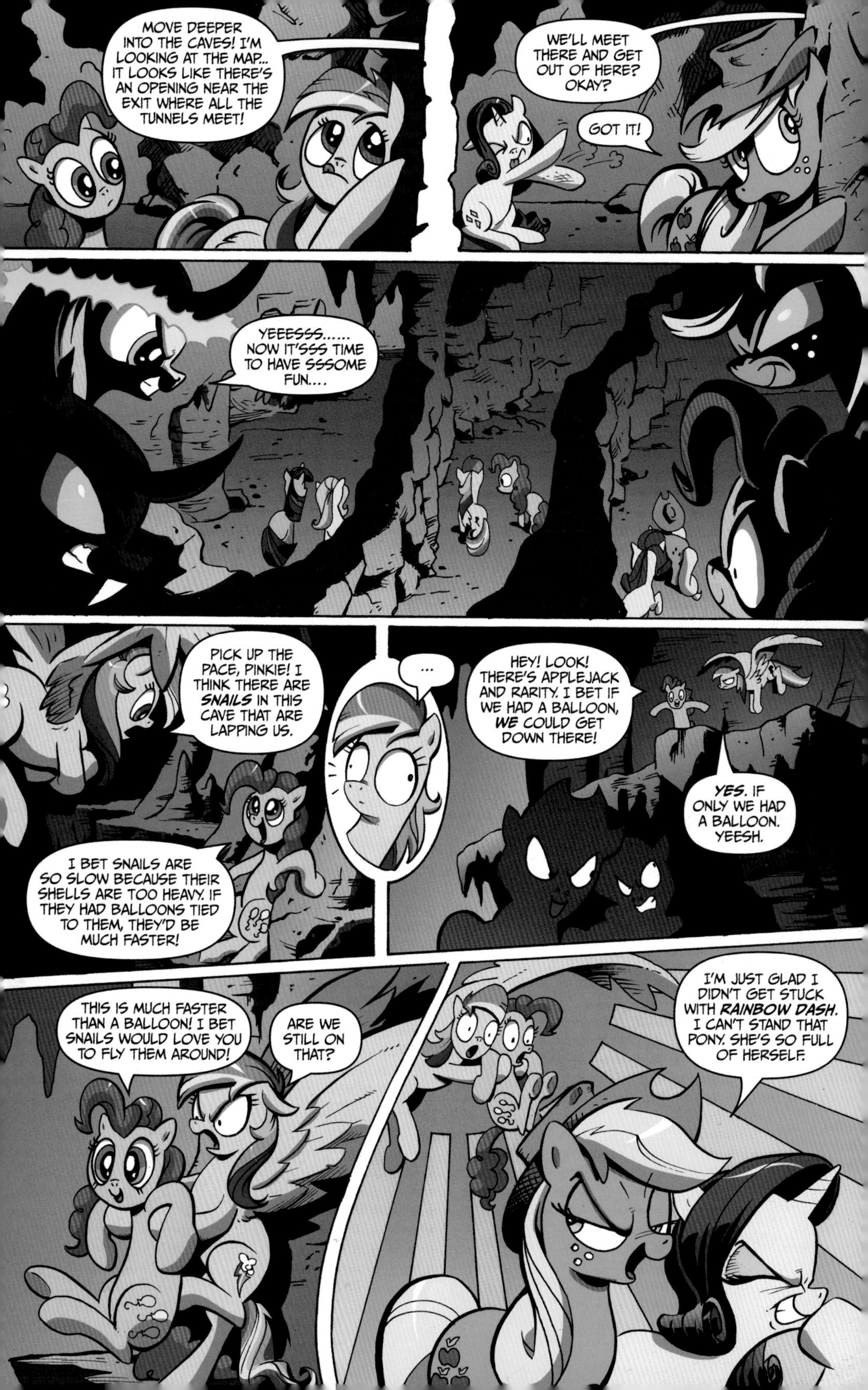
MOVE DEEPER INTO THE CAVES! I'M LOOKING AT THE MAP... IT LOOKS LIKE THERE'S AN OPENING NEAR THE EXIT WHERE ALL THE TUNNELS MEET!
WE'LL MEET THERE AND GET OUT OF HERE? OKAY?
GOT IT!
YEEESSS...... NOW IT'SSS TIME TO HAVE SSSOME FUN....
PICK UP THE PACE, PINKIE! I THINK THERE ARE SNAILS IN THIS CAVE THAT ARE LAPPING US.
I BET SNAILS ARE SO SLOW BECAUSE THEIR SHELLS ARE TOO HEAVY. IF THEY HAD BALLOONS TIED TO THEM, THEY'D BE MUCH FASTER!
...
HEY! LOOK! THERE'S APPLEJACK AND RARITY. I BET IF WE HAD A BALLOON, WE COULD GET DOWN THERE!
YES. IF ONLY WE HAD A BALLOON. YEESH.
THIS IS MUCH FASTER THAN A BALLOON! I BET SNAILS WOULD LOVE YOU TO FLY THEM AROUND!
ARE WE STILL ON THAT?
I'M JUST GLAD I DIDN'T GET STUCK WITH RAINBOW DASH. I CAN'T STAND THAT PONY. SHE'S SO FULL OF HERSELF.

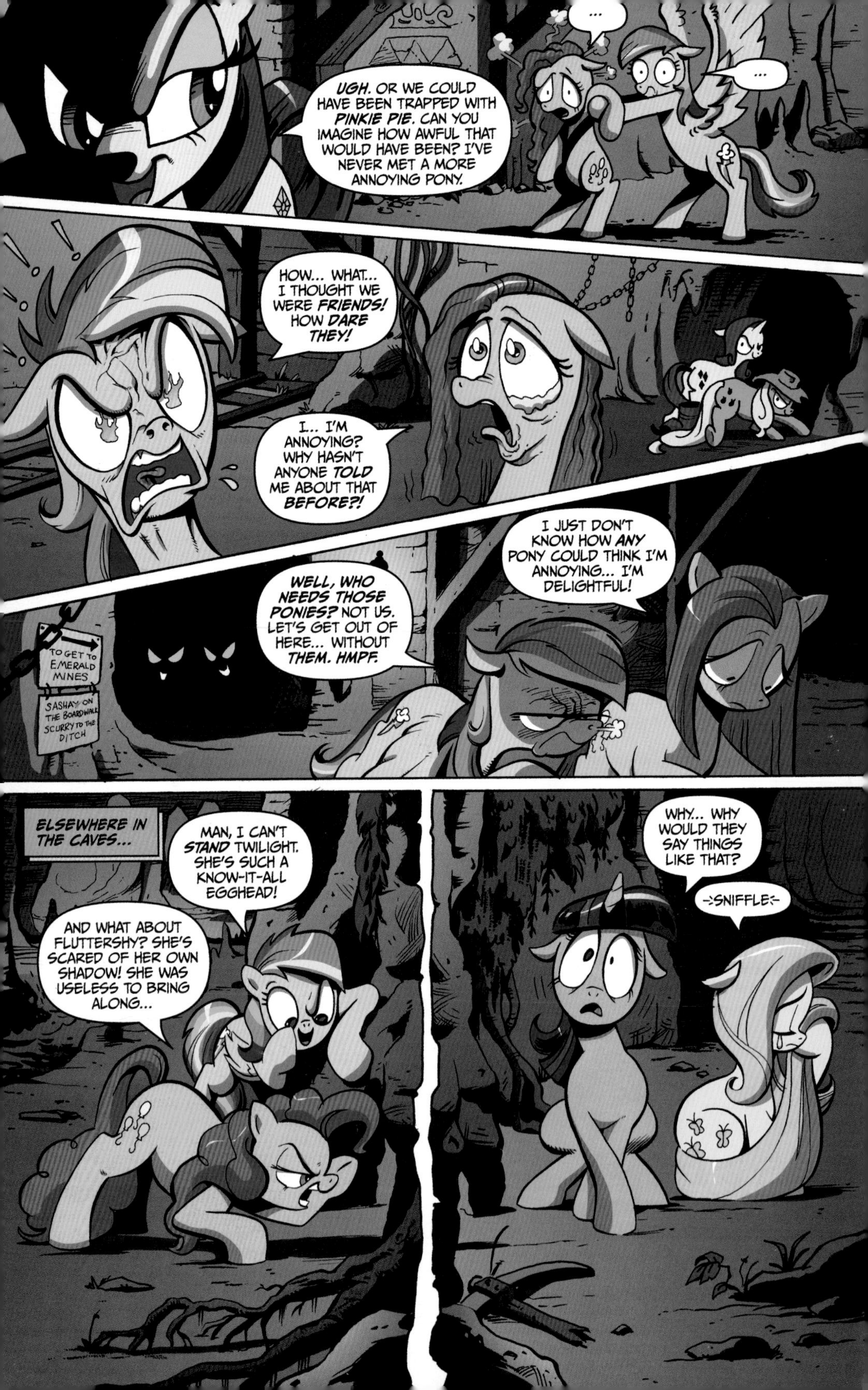
...
UGH. OR WE COULD HAVE BEEN TRAPPED WITH PINKIE PIE. CAN YOU IMAGINE HOW AWFUL THAT WOULD HAVE BEEN? I'VE NEVER MET A MORE ANNOYING PONY.
...
HOW... WHAT... I THOUGHT WE WERE FRIENDS! HOW DARE THEY!
I... I'M ANNOYING? WHY HASN'T ANYONE TOLD ME ABOUT THAT BEFORE?!
TO GET TO EMERALD MINES
SASHAY ON THE BOARDWALK SCURRY TO THE DITCH
WELL, WHO NEEDS THOSE PONIES? NOT US. LET'S GET OUT OF HERE... WITHOUT THEM. HMPF.
I JUST DON'T KNOW HOW ANY PONY COULD THINK I'M ANNOYING... I'M DELIGHTFUL!
ELSEWHERE IN THE CAVES...
MAN, I CAN'T STAND TWILIGHT. SHE'S SUCH A KNOW-IT-ALL EGGHEAD!
AND WHAT ABOUT FLUTTERSHY? SHE'S SCARED OF HER OWN SHADOW! SHE WAS USELESS TO BRING ALONG...
WHY... WHY WOULD THEY SAY THINGS LIKE THAT?
SNIFFLE

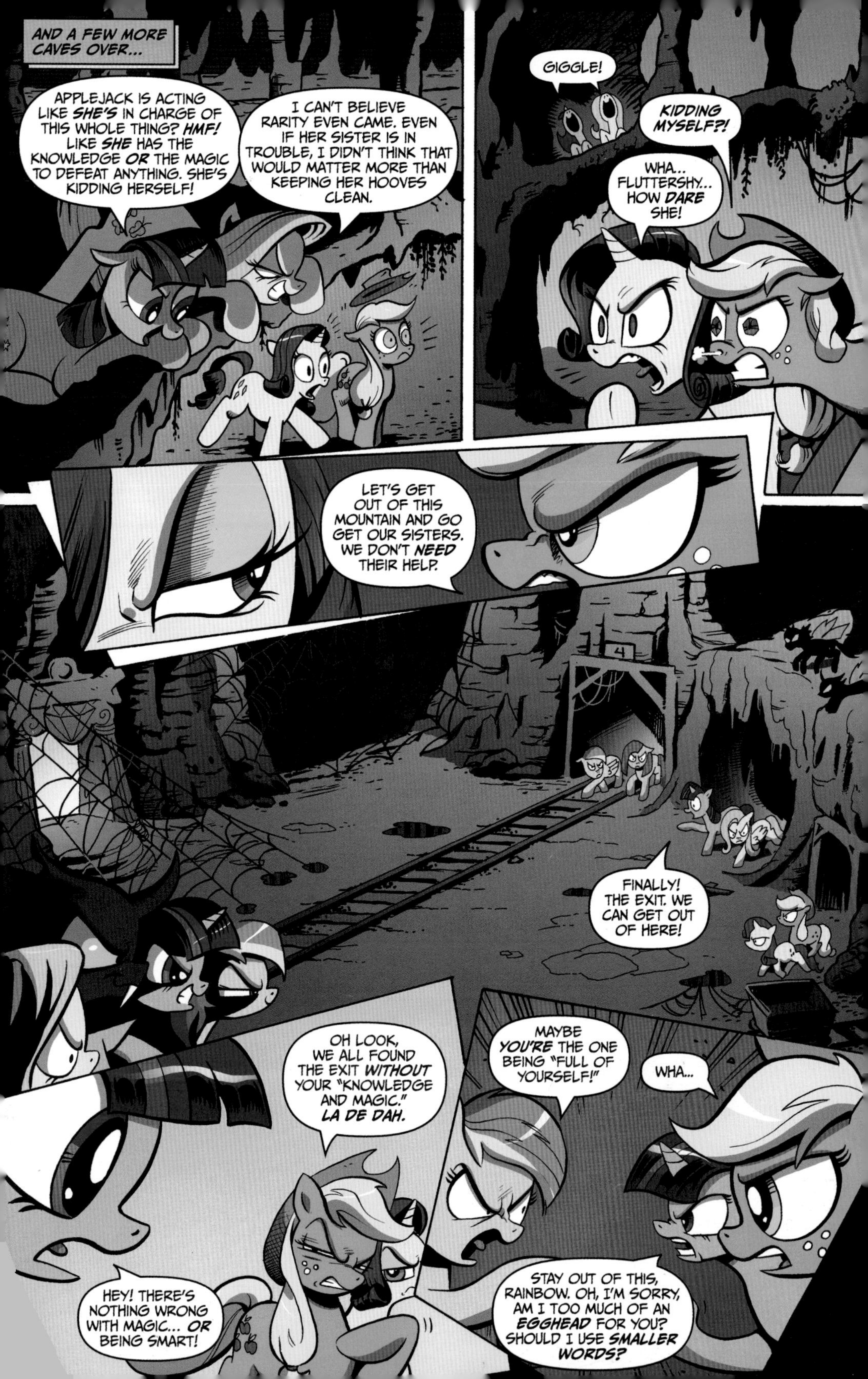
AND A FEW MORE CAVES OVER...
APPLEJACK IS ACTING LIKE SHE'S IN CHARGE OF THIS WHOLE THING? HMF! LIKE SHE HAS THE KNOWLEDGE OR THE MAGIC TO DEFEAT ANYTHING. SHE'S KIDDING HERSELF!
I CAN'T BELIEVE RARITY EVEN CAME. EVEN IF HER SISTER IS IN TROUBLE, I DIDN'T THINK THAT WOULD MATTER MORE THAN KEEPING HER HOOVES CLEAN.
GIGGLE!
KIDDING MYSELF?!
WHA... FLUTTERSHY... HOW DARE SHE!
LET'S GET OUT OF THIS MOUNTAIN AND GO GET OUR SISTERS. WE DON'T NEED THEIR HELP.
4
FINALLY! THE EXIT. WE CAN GET OUT OF HERE!
OH LOOK, WE ALL FOUND THE EXIT WITHOUT YOUR "KNOWLEDGE AND MAGIC." LA DE DAH.
MAYBE YOU'RE THE ONE BEING "FULL OF YOURSELF!"
WHA...
HEY! THERE'S NOTHING WRONG WITH MAGIC... OR BEING SMART!
STAY OUT OF THIS, RAINBOW. OH, I'M SORRY, AM I TOO MUCH OF AN EGGHEAD FOR YOU? SHOULD I USE SMALLER WORDS?

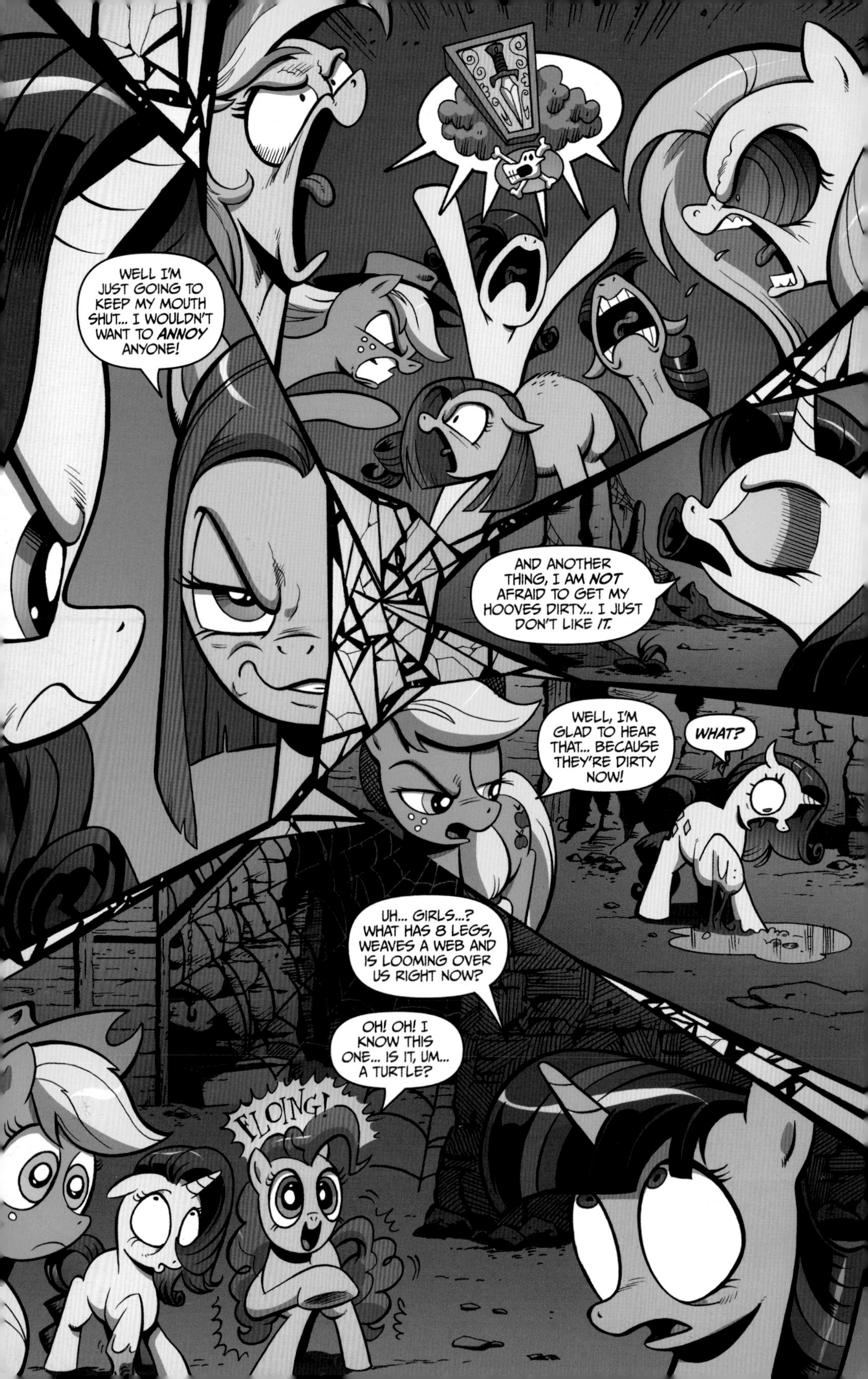
WELL I'M JUST GOING TO KEEP MY MOUTH SHUT... I WOULDN'T WANT TO *ANNOY* ANYONE!
AND ANOTHER THING, I AM ***NOT*** AFRAID TO GET MY HOOVES DIRTY... I JUST DON'T LIKE *IT.*
WELL, I'M GLAD TO HEAR THAT... BECAUSE THEY'RE DIRTY NOW!
WHAT?
UH... GIRLS...? WHAT HAS 8 LEGS, WEAVES A WEB AND IS LOOMING OVER US RIGHT NOW?
OH! OH! I KNOW THIS ONE... IS IT, UM... A TURTLE?
FLOING!

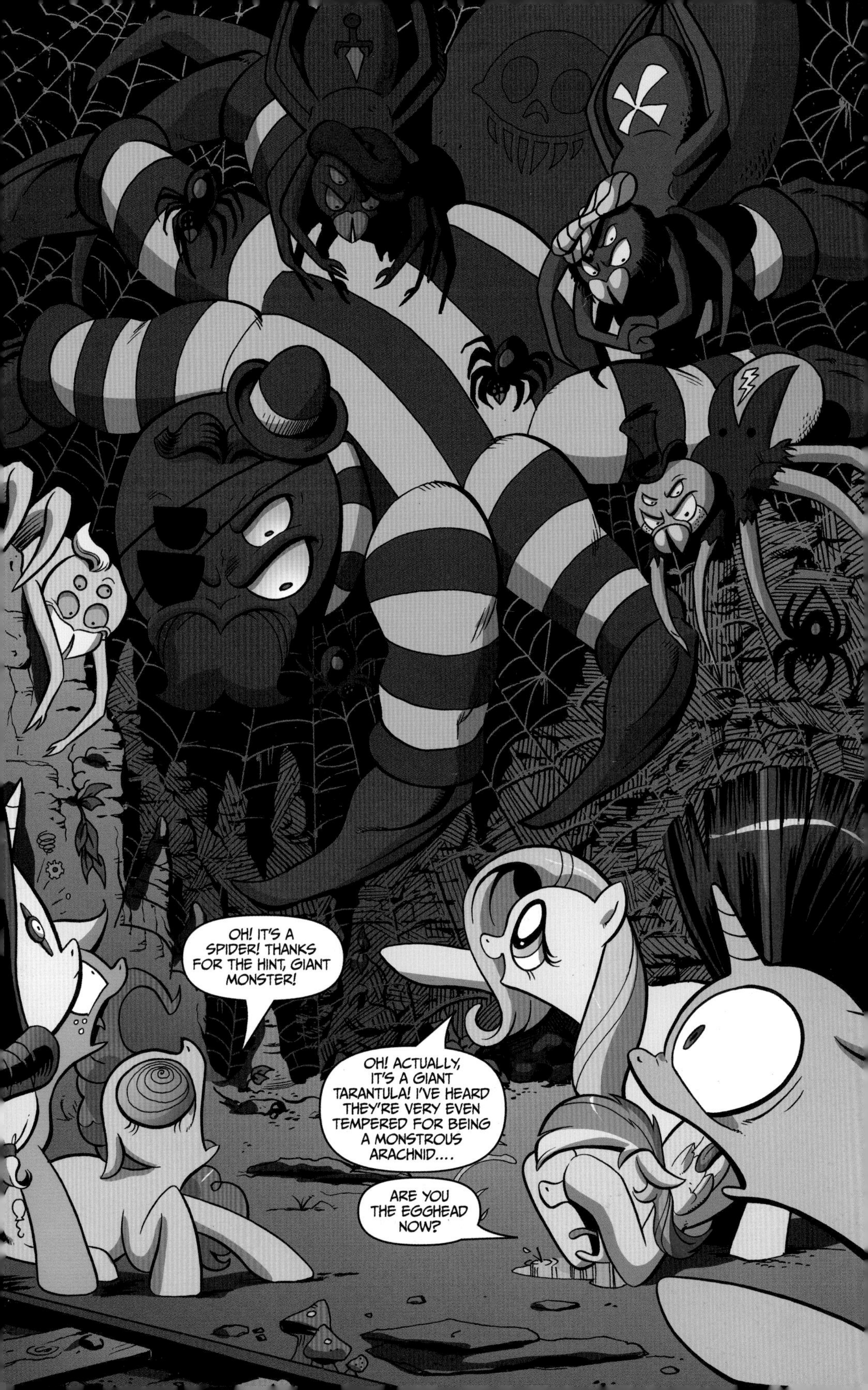
OH! IT'S A SPIDER! THANKS FOR THE HINT, GIANT MONSTER!
OH! ACTUALLY, IT'S A GIANT TARANTULA! I'VE HEARD THEY'RE VERY EVEN TEMPERED FOR BEING A MONSTROUS ARACHNID....
ARE YOU THE EGGHEAD NOW?

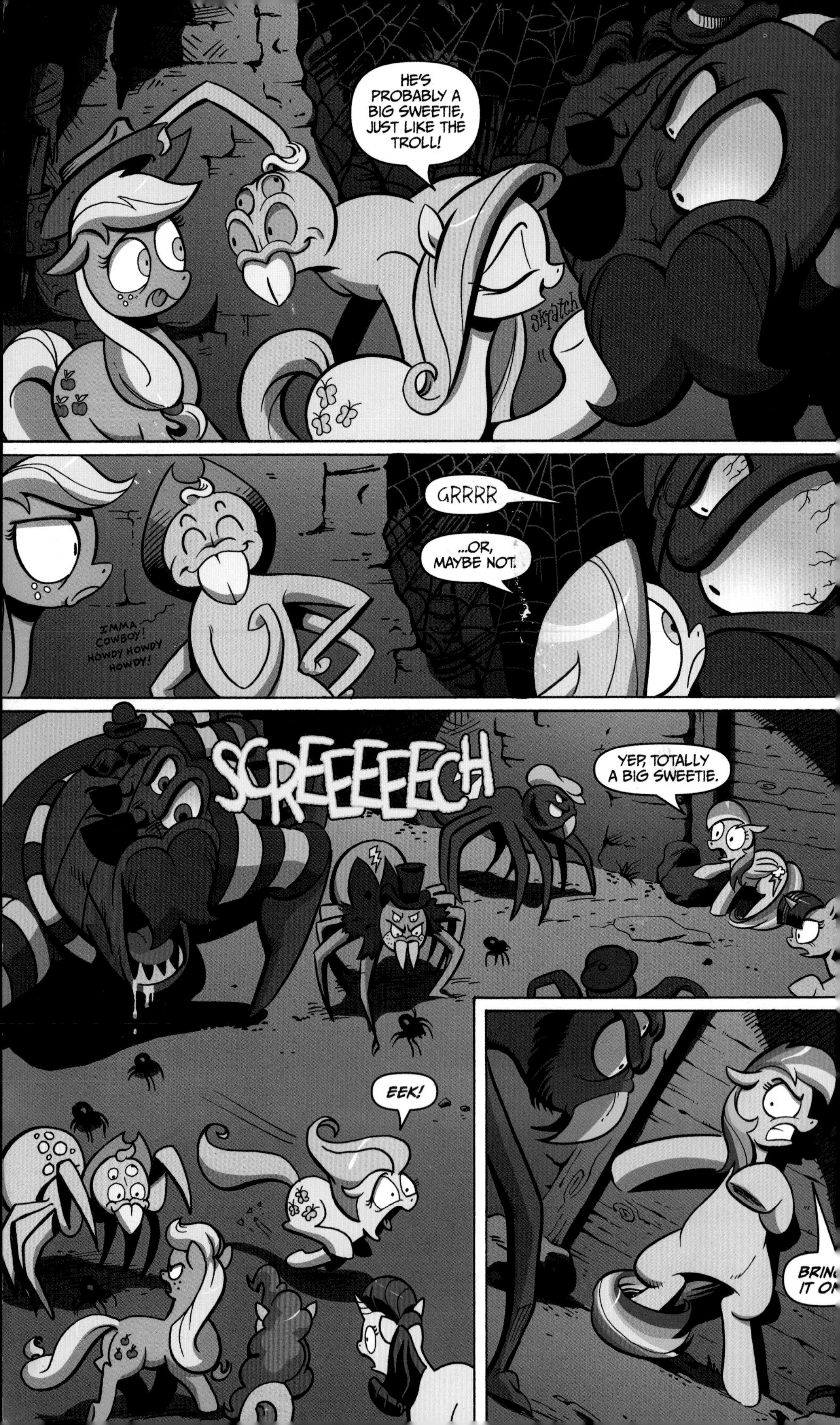
HE'S PROBABLY A BIG SWEETIE, JUST LIKE THE TROLL!
Skratch
GRRRR
...OR, MAYBE NOT.
IMMA COWBOY! HOWDY HOWDY HOWDY!
SCREEEEECH
YEP, TOTALLY A BIG SWEETIE.
EEK!
BRIN
IT O

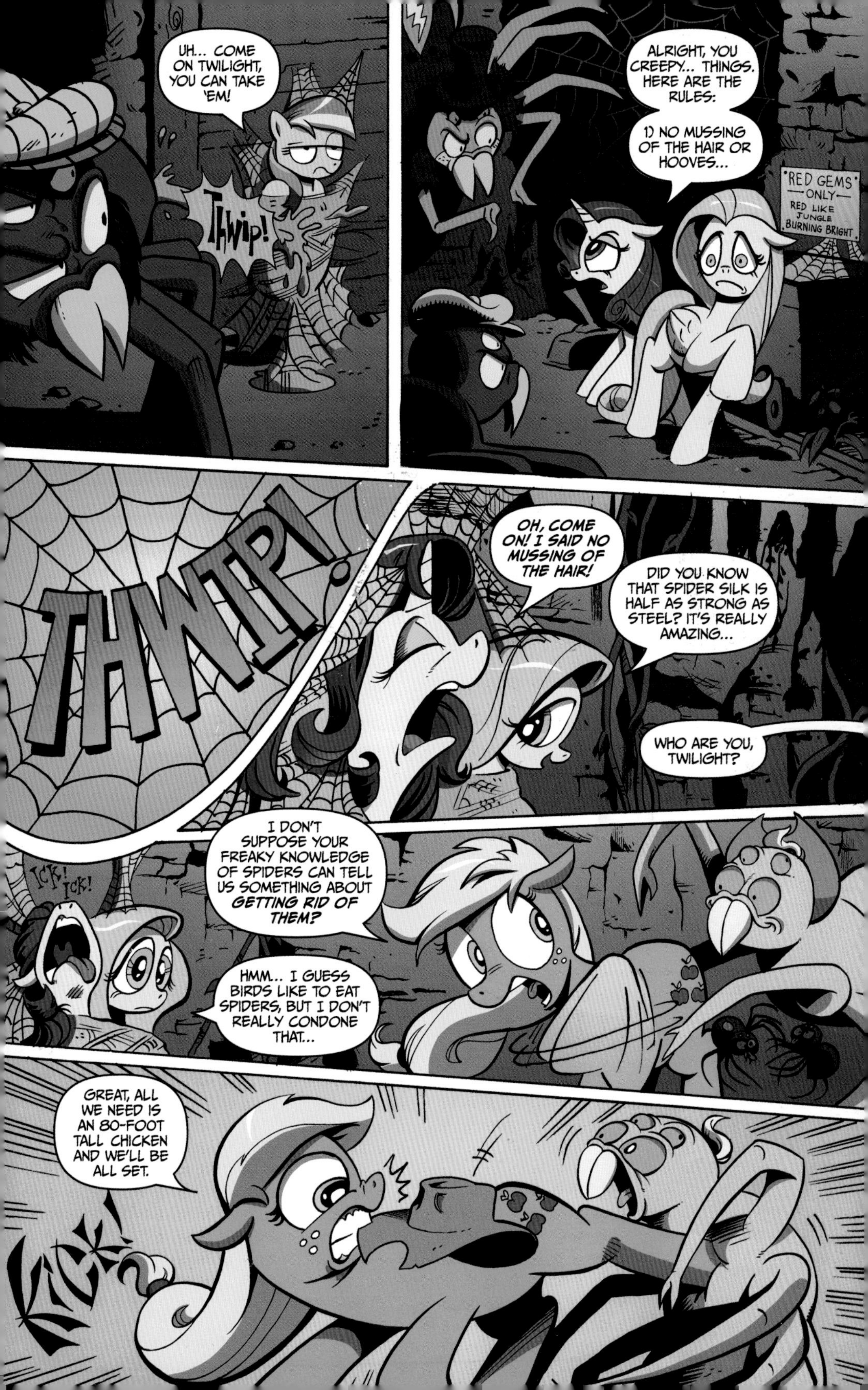

UH... COME ON TWILIGHT, YOU CAN TAKE 'EM!
THWIP!
ALRIGHT, YOU CREEPY... THINGS. HERE ARE THE RULES:
1) NO MUSSING OF THE HAIR OR HOOVES...
RED GEMS ONLY
RED LIKE JUNGLE BURNING BRIGHT
THWIP!
OH, COME ON! I SAID NO MUSSING OF THE HAIR!
DID YOU KNOW THAT SPIDER SILK IS HALF AS STRONG AS STEEL? IT'S REALLY AMAZING...
WHO ARE YOU, TWILIGHT?
ICK! ICK!
I DON'T SUPPOSE YOUR FREAKY KNOWLEDGE OF SPIDERS CAN TELL US SOMETHING ABOUT GETTING RID OF THEM?
HMM... I GUESS BIRDS LIKE TO EAT SPIDERS, BUT I DON'T REALLY CONDONE THAT...
GREAT, ALL WE NEED IS AN 80-FOOT TALL CHICKEN AND WE'LL BE ALL SET.
KICK!

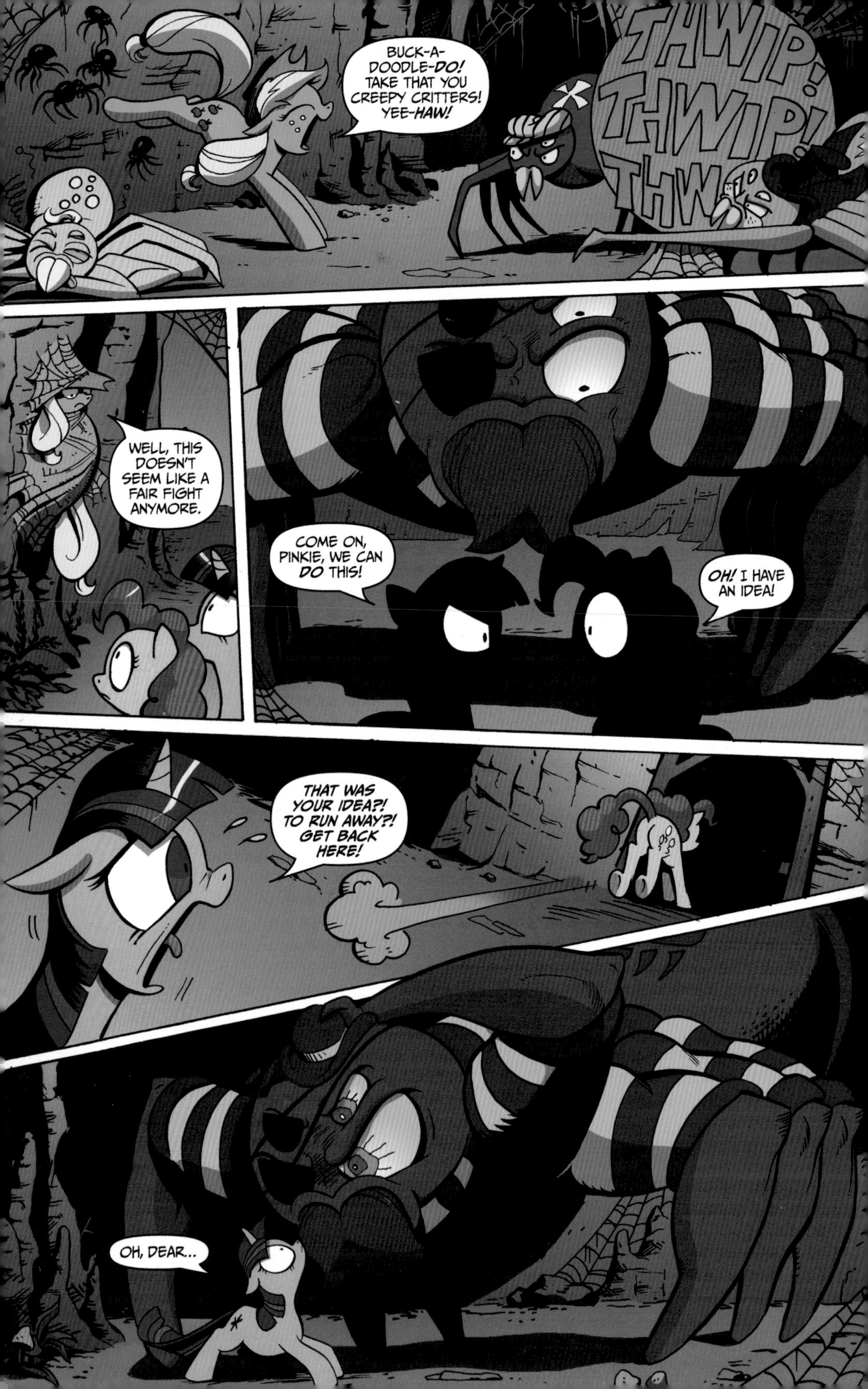
BUCK-A-DOODLE-DO! TAKE THAT YOU CREEPY CRITTERS! YEE-HAW!
THWIP! THWIP! THW
WELL, THIS DOESN'T SEEM LIKE A FAIR FIGHT ANYMORE.
COME ON, PINKIE, WE CAN DO THIS!
OH! I HAVE AN IDEA!
THAT WAS YOUR IDEA?! TO RUN AWAY?! GET BACK HERE!
OH, DEAR...

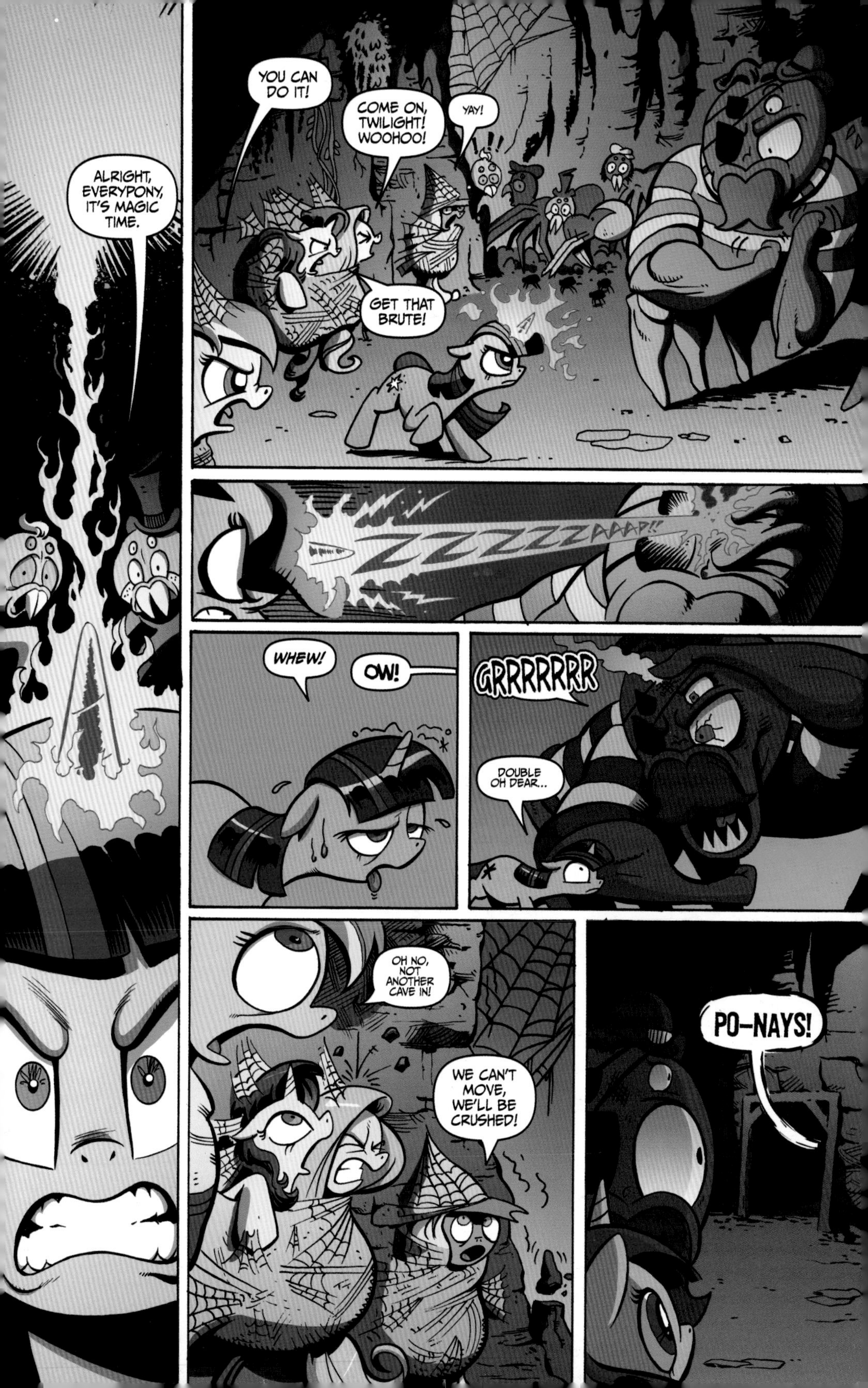
ALRIGHT, EVERYPONY, IT'S MAGIC TIME.
YOU CAN DO IT!
COME ON, TWILIGHT! WOOHOO!
YAY!
GET THAT BRUTE!
ZZZZZZAAAP!!
WHEW!
OW!
GRRRRRRR
DOUBLE OH DEAR...
OH NO, NOT ANOTHER CAVE IN!
WE CAN'T MOVE, WE'LL BE CRUSHED!
PO-NAYS!

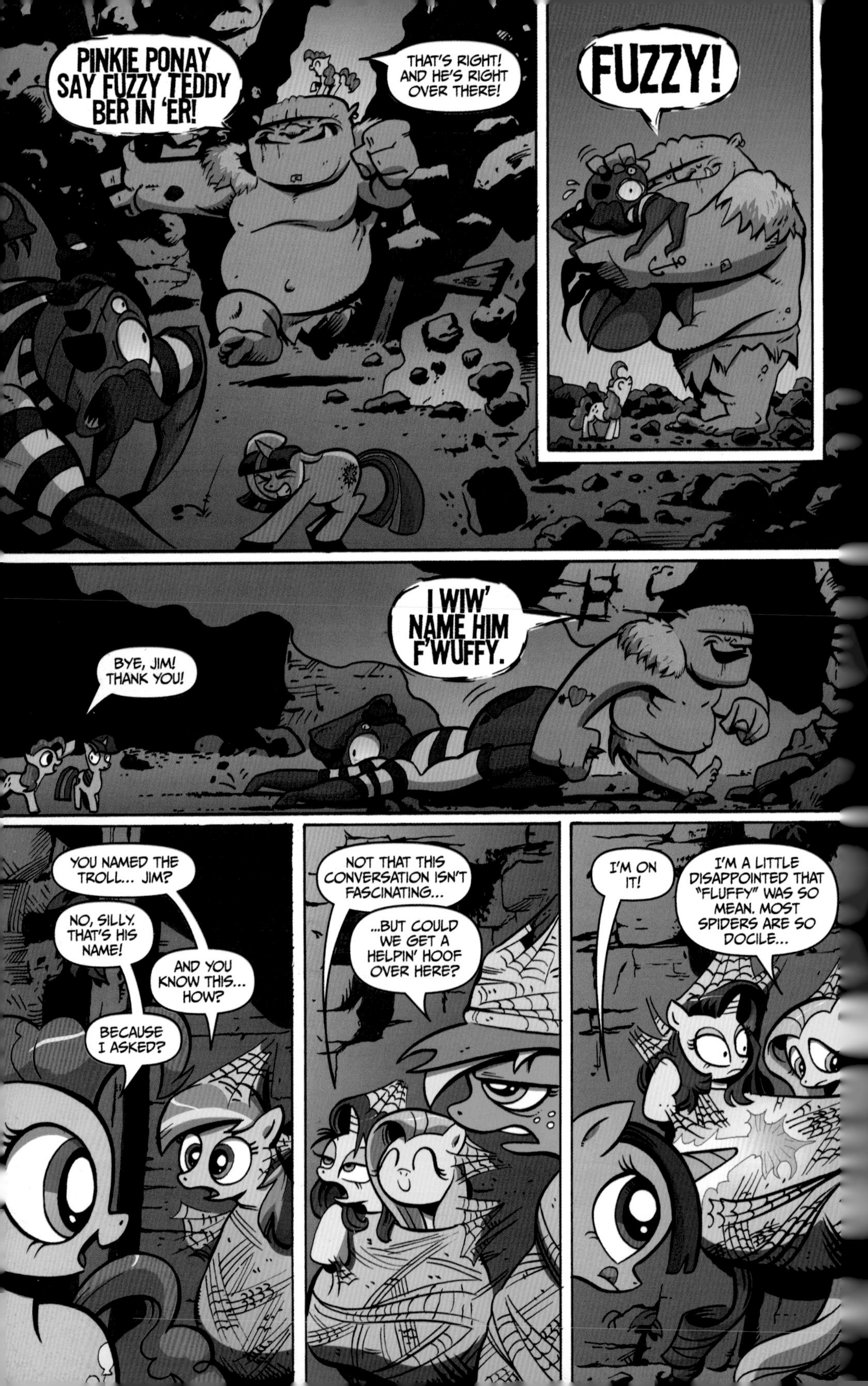
PINKIE PONAY SAY FUZZY TEDDY BER IN 'ER!
THAT'S RIGHT! AND HE'S RIGHT OVER THERE!
FUZZY!
I WIW' NAME HIM F'WUFFY.
BYE, JIM! THANK YOU!
YOU NAMED THE TROLL... JIM?
NO, SILLY. THAT'S HIS NAME!
AND YOU KNOW THIS... HOW?
BECAUSE I ASKED?
NOT THAT THIS CONVERSATION ISN'T FASCINATING...
...BUT COULD WE GET A HELPIN' HOOF OVER HERE?
I'M ON IT!
I'M A LITTLE DISAPPOINTED THAT "FLUFFY" WAS SO MEAN. MOST SPIDERS ARE SO DOCILE...

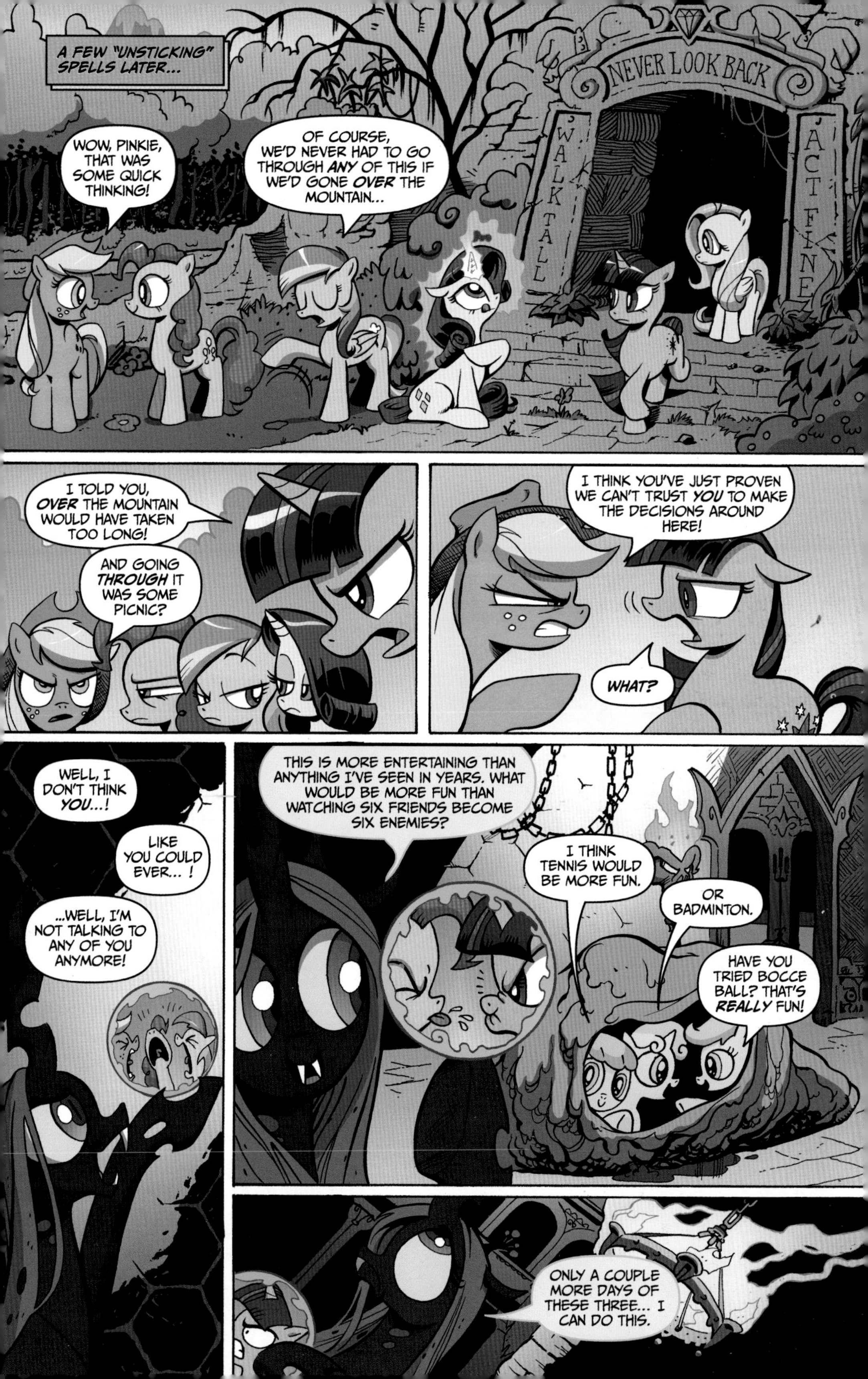
A FEW "UNSTICKING" SPELLS LATER...
NEVER LOOK BACK
WALK TALL
ACT FINE
WOW, PINKIE, THAT WAS SOME QUICK THINKING!
OF COURSE, WE'D NEVER HAD TO GO THROUGH ANY OF THIS IF WE'D GONE OVER THE MOUNTAIN...
I TOLD YOU, OVER THE MOUNTAIN WOULD HAVE TAKEN TOO LONG!
AND GOING THROUGH IT WAS SOME PICNIC?
I THINK YOU'VE JUST PROVEN WE CAN'T TRUST YOU TO MAKE THE DECISIONS AROUND HERE!
WHAT?
WELL, I DON'T THINK YOU...!
LIKE YOU COULD EVER... !
...WELL, I'M NOT TALKING TO ANY OF YOU ANYMORE!
THIS IS MORE ENTERTAINING THAN ANYTHING I'VE SEEN IN YEARS. WHAT WOULD BE MORE FUN THAN WATCHING SIX FRIENDS BECOME SIX ENEMIES?
I THINK TENNIS WOULD BE MORE FUN.
OR BADMINTON.
HAVE YOU TRIED BOCCE BALL? THAT'S REALLY FUN!
ONLY A COUPLE MORE DAYS OF THESE THREE... I CAN DO THIS.

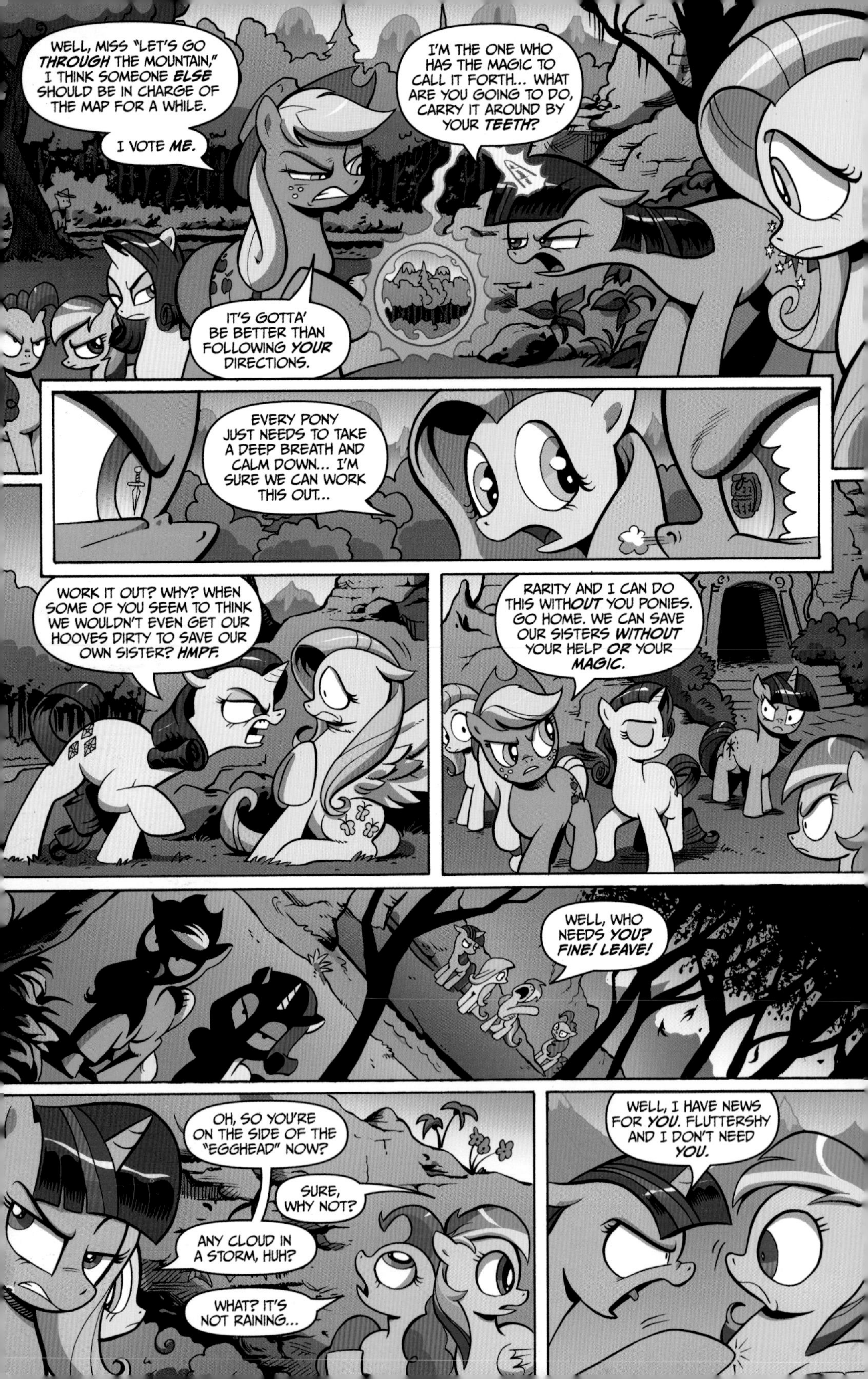

WELL, MISS "LET'S GO THROUGH THE MOUNTAIN," I THINK SOMEONE ELSE SHOULD BE IN CHARGE OF THE MAP FOR A WHILE.
I VOTE ME.
I'M THE ONE WHO HAS THE MAGIC TO CALL IT FORTH... WHAT ARE YOU GOING TO DO, CARRY IT AROUND BY YOUR TEETH?
IT'S GOTTA' BE BETTER THAN FOLLOWING YOUR DIRECTIONS.
EVERY PONY JUST NEEDS TO TAKE A DEEP BREATH AND CALM DOWN... I'M SURE WE CAN WORK THIS OUT...
WORK IT OUT? WHY? WHEN SOME OF YOU SEEM TO THINK WE WOULDN'T EVEN GET OUR HOOVES DIRTY TO SAVE OUR OWN SISTER? HMPF.
RARITY AND I CAN DO THIS WITHOUT YOU PONIES. GO HOME. WE CAN SAVE OUR SISTERS WITHOUT YOUR HELP OR YOUR MAGIC.
WELL, WHO NEEDS YOU? FINE! LEAVE!
OH, SO YOU'RE ON THE SIDE OF THE "EGGHEAD" NOW?
SURE, WHY NOT?
ANY CLOUD IN A STORM, HUH?
WHAT? IT'S NOT RAINING...
WELL, I HAVE NEWS FOR YOU. FLUTTERSHY AND I DON'T NEED YOU.

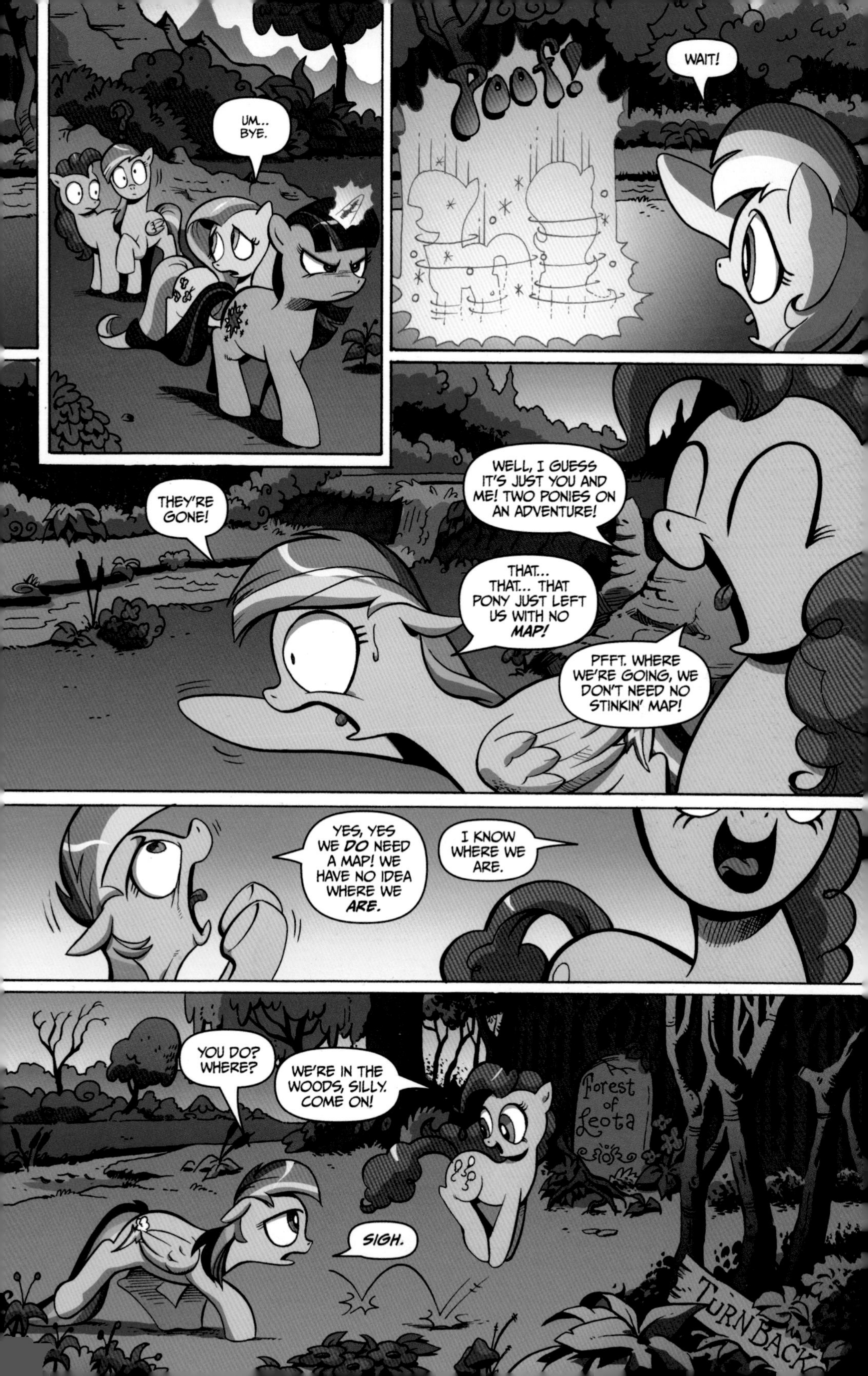
UM.. BYE.
POOF!
WAIT!
THEY'RE GONE!
WELL, I GUESS IT'S JUST YOU AND ME! TWO PONIES ON AN ADVENTURE!
THAT... THAT... THAT PONY JUST LEFT US WITH NO *MAP!*
PFFT. WHERE WE'RE GOING, WE DON'T NEED NO STINKIN' MAP!
YES, YES WE *DO* NEED A MAP! WE HAVE NO IDEA WHERE WE *ARE.*
I KNOW WHERE WE ARE.
YOU DO? WHERE?
WE'RE IN THE WOODS, SILLY. COME ON!
Forest of Leota
SIGH.
TURN BACK

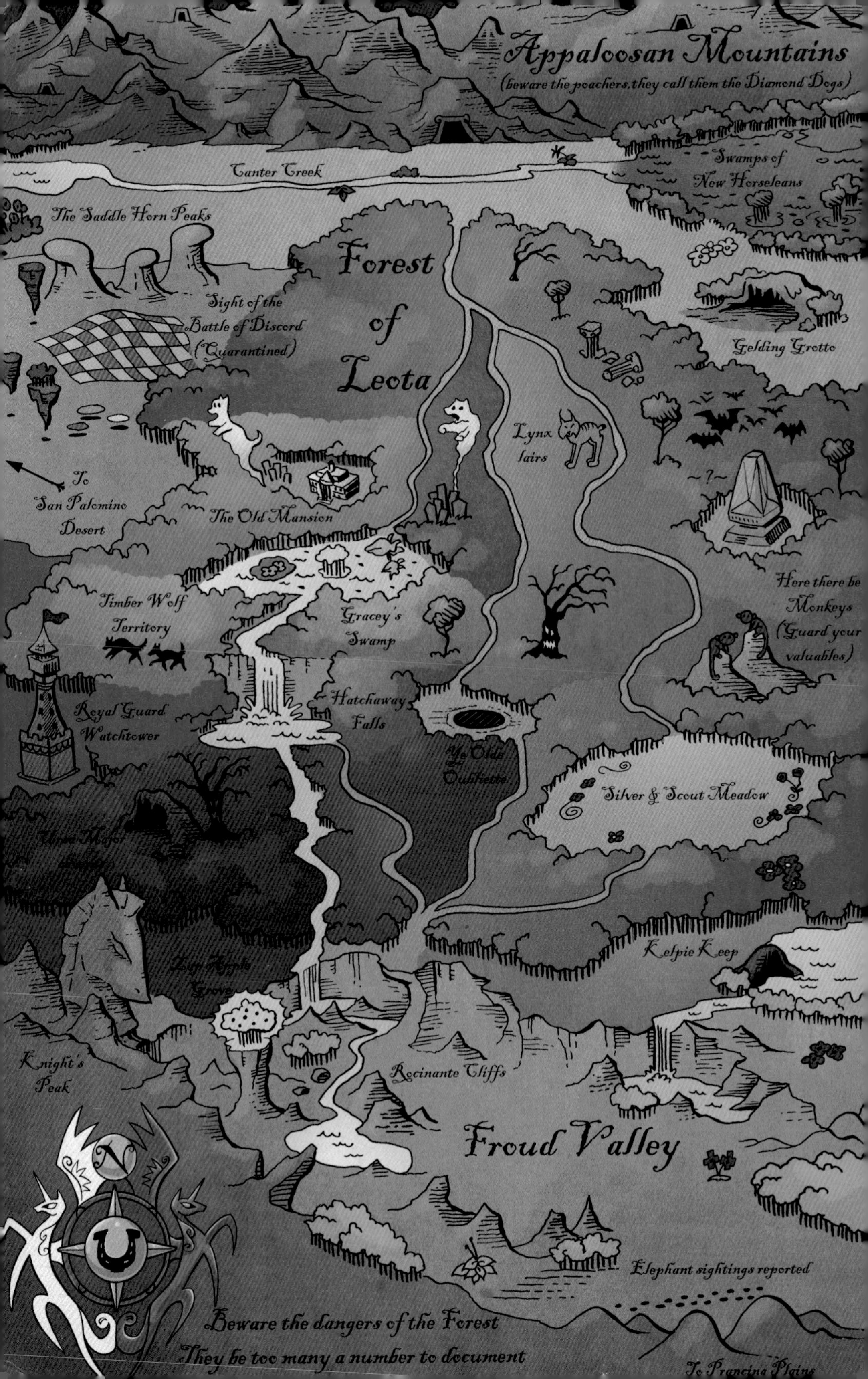

Appaloosan Mountains
(beware the poachers, they call them the Diamond Dogs)
Canter Creek
Swamps of New Horseleans
The Saddle Horn Peaks
Forest of Leota
Sight of the Battle of Discord (Quarantined)
Gelding Grotto
Lynx lairs
To San Palomino Desert
The Old Mansion
~?~
Timber Wolf Territory
Gracey's Swamp
Here there be Monkeys (Guard your valuables)
Hatchaway Falls
Royal Guard Watchtower
Ye Olde Oubliette
Silver & Scout Meadow
Ursa Major
Zap Apple Grove
Kelpie Keep
Knight's Peak
Rocinante Cliffs
Froud Valley
Elephant sightings reported
Beware the dangers of the Forest
They be too many a number to document
To Prancing Plains

my LITTLE PONY™
Friendship is Magic

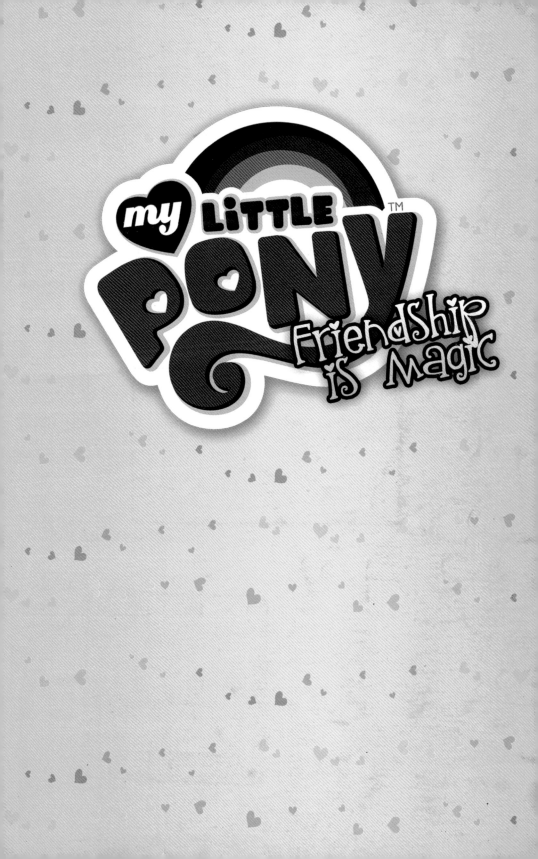

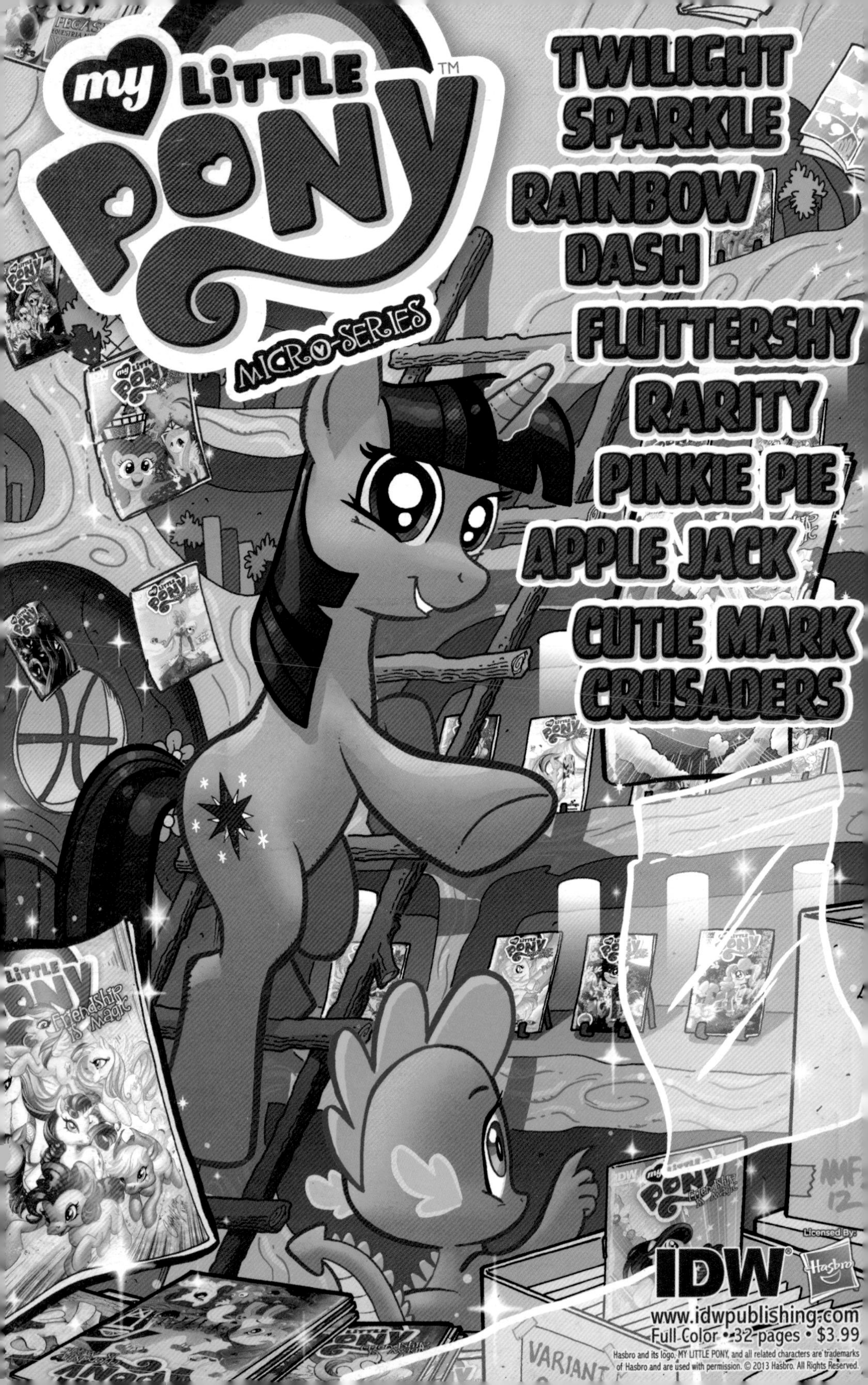

my LITTLE PONY™
MICRO-SERIES
TWILIGHT SPARKLE
RAINBOW DASH
FLUTTERSHY
RARITY
PINKIE PIE
APPLE JACK
CUTIE MARK CRUSADERS
Licensed By:
IDW®
Hasbro
www.idwpublishing.com
Full Color • 32 pages • $3.99
Hasbro and its logo, MY LITTLE PONY, and all related characters are trademarks of Hasbro and are used with permission. © 2013 Hasbro. All Rights Reserved.